TOUCHDOWN ON LOVE

A Texas Tornado Romance

LORANA HOOPES

To my wonderful readers who inspire me to write every day.
To my father who got me into watching football when I was young.
To Emmitt Smith who was my favorite ball player of all time. He had so much class, and I loved how he finished his degree as well. Such an inspiration!
To all the first responders who are working so hard during this Covid-19 crisis.

CLARA

Clara Bradford stared at the meticulously typed letter in disbelief. Yes, she had applied, but she hadn't really expected to get an interview. After all, the Tornadoes were National Champions, and she was just one of the athletic trainers for a local university. True, it was one of the larger, more well-known universities and she had helped rehabilitate several up and coming athletes, but there had to have been hundreds of qualified applicants.

"Is that what I think it is?" Her friend and fellow trainer, Stacy Givens, asked as she leaned over her shoulder to read the paper. It had been Stacy's idea for Clara to apply. The girl was always pushing her to do more, challenge herself. Well, she'd certainly done it this time.

"It is. They want to interview me." Clara could only blink

at the words inviting her to come to Southlake for an interview.

Stacy's arms wrapped around her and squeezed so tightly that Clara felt like a grape in a vise. "I knew it. I don't want to say I told you so, but I told you so." A look of satisfaction covered her face.

Clara chuckled at those words. Stacy enjoyed being right, so being able to say "I told you so" was definitely something she wanted to say. The only problem was, she didn't know about Clara's past. Stacy didn't know that Clara's ex-boyfriend was a wide receiver for the Texas Tornadoes. Could she really work on his team knowing that she would have to see him? And what if he got injured? Would she be able to watch him get hit again and again? Even more importantly could she work that closely with him? Would he even let her?

Stacy stepped back from Clara and crossed her arms. One eyebrow arched on her forehead as she fixed Clara with a questioning look. "Okay, what's going on? You should be ecstatic about this interview yet pensive and hesitant are more the vibes I'm getting from you."

Clara bit her lip as she debated if she wanted to share this story with Stacy. Yes, they had been friends for the last few years, having gone through the same program in college and then ending up on the same college team, but this was not something she was proud of. This was her biggest regret and the one thing she would change if she could go back in time. She decided sharing part of the truth would be okay. "I used to date one of the players on the Tornadoes."

Stacy's eyes widened and her mouth dropped open. "You did? Which one?"

"Mason Dixon."

A confused expression clouded Stacy's face. "Like the boundary line that separates Pennsylvania and Maryland?"

Clara chuckled as she remembered how many times she'd had to answer a similar question in the past. "No, like the wide receiver for the Tornadoes, but yes, like the line. His parents have an odd sense of humor."

"So, who broke it off?" Stacy's eyebrow lifted again as she leaned back and crossed her arms.

Boy if that wasn't a long story, but that was the part of the story Clara wasn't going to go into right now. "I guess I did, sort of."

A knowing look covered Stacy's face, and she nodded. "And you're worried... what? That you'll fall for him again?"

That was exactly what she was worried about, among other things. "No, not really. It's been a few years."

"So, you're worried that he's found someone else?"

Well, now she was. She hadn't even thought of that possibility until it crossed Stacy's lips. Could she watch him date another woman? What if he had already found one and was married? What if he already had kids? "I don't know exactly what I'm worried about. I guess that it might be weird, that he might not want to work with me."

That no-nonsense look took over Stacy's face. It was the same one she used whenever guys tried to say women couldn't work with football players, and Clara loved it. Normally. "Honey, I'm sure he's a professional. It's his job to work with whoever the team hires, and if that's you, then I'm sure he'll be fine.

Clara hoped Stacy was right. Of course, she didn't have the job yet, but this would be a huge stepping stone for her if she got it. She'd be crazy not to go to the interview, but then why did she feel like her life was about to get turned upside down?

THE TORNADO TRAINING FACILITY WAS HUGE, AND CLARA felt like a tiny fish in a big ocean as she walked up the sidewalk to the front door. She hoped they had a receptionist because she didn't want to get lost in this building. It would be just her luck to run into Mason while wandering around the place looking for the interview.

She needn't have worried though. A reception desk was the first thing she saw upon opening the door. Large and white, it filled a good portion of the room, and was manned by not one but two women with headsets attached to their ears.

"Can I help you?" the one on the right asked as Clara approached. Though her blonde hair was pulled back and sprayed, a kind smile resided on her face, and her eyes were friendly.

"Yes, I'm Clara Bradford. I have an interview for the athletic trainer position."

The woman nodded and clicked a few buttons on her computer before looking up again. "I have you all checked in, Ms. Bradford. You may sit over there until you are called back." She pointed to a sitting area that looked more like a living room with a comfy couch, a few chairs, and a lamp on a table.

"Thank you." Clara returned the woman's smile and then walked over to the chairs. As she sat, she pulled out her phone. Might as well get some reading done while she waited. Though she generally preferred holding a paperback, it was nice to have access to books on her phone and equally nice that it held her place for her.

She had just reached the most interesting part of the book when she heard her name being called. Stifling a frustrated sigh, she stood and pocketed the phone. She'd have to finish the book later. Her hand smoothed her skirt, and with a smile pasted on her face, she approached the man who had called her.

He held a clipboard in his hand and was obviously on the athletic team if his attire choice of joggers and a t-shirt with the team logo on it was any indication, but he looked young.

She wondered if he was even old enough to be out of college. An intern then?

"I'm Clara." She held her hand out, and after a moment and a confused expression, the man shifted his clipboard to his other arm in order to return her shake.

"Neal, but I'm just the intern. If you'll follow me, I'll take you to the interview room."

Clara felt a heat color her cheeks, but it never hurt to butter up interns. She'd been one herself once, and she always appreciated the people who took the time to learn her name and treat her like a person. "How long have you been interning?"

"This is my first year, but it's been great. The doctors are good people to work with and most of the players are pretty down to earth."

She knew what he meant with his carefully chosen words. She'd worked with some amazing players, but there were a few who seemed to have a "god" complex and thought they were the best thing since sliced bread. Those were the ones who were hard to work with because they always thought they knew best and often ignored her suggestions. It was less noticeable at the college level where she was currently working, but having seen it with a few of those guys, she could only imagine how much worse it must get when people were getting paid millions to play.

"Here we are," he said, stopping in front of a simple yet imposing brown door. "Good luck."

"Thank you." Clara flashed him a smile and then squared her shoulders before pushing the door open. The room inside was a conference type room with a long rectangular table. Four older men were seated around the table, and at the sound of the door opening, their eyes lifted to stare back at her. Though she was used to working only with men, she had hoped to see a woman in the department. Of course, this might not be the whole department.

"Ms. Bradford, I assume?" one of the men asked after looking down at his clipboard.

"Yes, I'm Clara Bradford." She flashed her best smile at the men, hoping she looked more confident than she felt, but none of them returned the emotion. Her courage faltered, and she glanced around for some clue as to what she was supposed to do next.

"You can take a seat," the man said, pointing to the chair at the head of the table.

"Of course, thank you." Clara pulled the chair out and sat down. Unsure of where to put her hands, she folded them in her lap and waited.

"So, tell us why you applied to the Tornadoes." Clara assumed this man must be the one in charge as he appeared to be leading the interview and the only one capable of speaking.

"Well, as I'm sure you know from my resume and application, I am currently an athletic trainer for the University of

Texas. I love my job, but I've always wanted to work for a professional team."

"For the notoriety?" the man asked, cutting her off. "Or the money?"

She blinked at him, blindsided by his assumptive question. "Neither. I grew up watching football with my dad. Since the age of four, it was the one thing we would do together every Sunday." She paused as she thought about the rest of her relationship with her father. Rocky would begin to describe it but just barely. "Since then, it's just been a dream of mine to help the players out, so I studied sports medicine, and," she shrugged, "here I am."

The man in charge eyed her, his gaze stern and unflinching as if he could discern the truth with his gaze. "All right. Well, being an athletic trainer for a professional team can be stressful. How do you handle stress and pressure?"

As long as it wasn't coming from her father, she handled it fine. "I handle stress and pressure very well. I make it a priority to work out to relieve my own stress, and as a believer, I take whatever I have to the Lord in prayer." She had no idea if these men were believers as well, but she wasn't about to hide the fact. After the breakup with Mason, God had been there for her, and she would not hide her love for Him.

The men exchanged glances, but Clara couldn't read their intent. "You do know most of our games are on Sundays which makes attending church challenging."

Clara smiled. She loved attending church on Sunday. There was something uplifting in the community aspect of it, but it wasn't the only way to have church and she still couldn't believe there were people who thought it was. "Matthew 18 says that church is wherever two or more are gathered in His name. My best friend lives just outside of town, so I'm fairly certain I'll be able to gather with her on days other than Sundays. In addition, I know there are several churches here in Southlake that offer Wednesday services, Saturday services, or even online services." She had done her homework when she had gotten the interview invitation.

The man nodded and rubbed a hand across his chin. "So they do. Okay, Ms. Bradford, one final question. Why should we hire you over all the other applicants we have?"

Clara paused. She hated questions like this because she was never sure how she was supposed to answer them. Did they want her to brag or be humble? "You should hire me because I'm good at what I do. I studied sports medicine extensively and have completed many additional training hours outside of what was needed for my degree. My passion for this is evident in everything I do, and my love for this game and for God shines through every day. I may be a woman in a predominantly man's field, but I don't back down easily." She tilted her chin up as if to punctuate her point, and, surprisingly, the man smiled back.

"I believe you there." The man stood and approached her,

extending a hand. "Obviously, we have several other qualified applicants, but we'll be in touch."

"Thank you." Clara shook his hand, making sure to keep
her grip firm as her father had taught her. Surprise flickered
across the man's face for just an instant before his grin
widened and he walked her to the door.

As it shut behind her, Clara couldn't help but think that
the job was hers. The interview had gone well, and a peace
filled her heart as if this was exactly where she was supposed
to be. She glanced at her watch as she headed for the parking
lot. It was still early. Perhaps Adrienne would have time for
an early dinner before she had to catch her flight home.

2

MASON

"Yes, Mom, I'm eating my vegetables." Mason shook his head as he cradled the cell phone with his shoulder, so he could open the locker. "The food is amazing. Remember I told you they hired a new cook?" He'd been over this with his mother when he'd first arrived at training camp last summer, but she still continued to pester him whenever he called.

"You just look so skinny on TV," she said.

"I'm a wide receiver, Mom. I run a lot." He had actually put on a few pounds due to the food, but he'd never be able to make his mother understand that. She only saw her little boy, and even though he was in his mid-twenties now, she still worried about him.

The locker room door opened, and the room filled with noise from his teammates. There was no way he was going to get caught on a call with his mother. One of the new recruits had done that earlier this year and the teasing had been merciless.

"Mom, I have to go. I'll call you later." He hung up before she could answer. He'd owe her a big apology later, but it was better than being caught on the phone with her.

"Mason, there you are. We were wondering where you ran off to." Blaine Hollis, quarterback and captain of the Tornadoes, opened his locker and pulled out a notebook. "Tucker and I thought maybe you'd snuck a girl back here."

"A girl?" Mason chuckled. He barely had time to date with the game schedule and his workouts, and even if he did, he wasn't sure he was ready. His last serious relationship had torn his heart wide open, and he wasn't sure it was mended enough to try again yet. "You two are more likely to sneak a woman back here."

Tucker, the team's star running back, had recently gotten married and Blaine had just proposed to his girlfriend, Kenzi. Mason was nowhere near that.

"He's got you there, Blaine," Tucker said as he grabbed a notebook from his locker as well. "But if you weren't in here with a girl, what were you doing?"

Mason swallowed, and his mind raced through plausible excuses. "I was calling the shop about my truck. It's been acting up lately, and I was hoping to get it looked at soon. I would have called from the cafeteria, but it was a little loud in there."

"Hard to be quiet when the food is so good," Jefferson said. Jefferson was another wide receiver, and he was an enigma to be sure. Though younger than almost everyone else on the team, he was solid and seemed to have this mature air about him, like he'd already seen the world.

"Has anybody met the cook yet?" Mason asked, grateful for the excuse to change the subject.

Jefferson shook his head. "Nope. They introduced the helpers, but she's always claimed she was too busy."

"I hear we're meeting the new athletic trainer today though," Tucker said.

Mason nodded as he grabbed his own notebook and followed the guys out of the locker room and toward the meeting room. One of their old trainers, Doug, had recently gotten married, and his bride had insisted they return to her home state of Alabama. Though he hadn't wanted to go, he'd wanted to stay married even more, and the team had been forced to send out an emergency notice for applications.

Mason was less than excited about meeting a new trainer. For one, he was pretty particular about who he worked with, and he had really liked Doug. The other reason was because of his ex-girlfriend, Clara. She had wanted to be an athletic trainer, and every time he had to meet a new one, it reminded him of her.

His mind wandered to her again as they walked down the hallway to the meeting room. Had she followed her dream? Was she working for some college team now? Or maybe even a professional team? She'd said that was her dream. For them to be on the same team - him playing ball and her stitching him up. That's what she'd said her dream was, but they must have been empty words because she'd broken up with him not long after that. He'd pressed her for the reason, but she had just shaken her head and said they were too different. Whatever that meant. So, he'd left.

He'd joined the Tornadoes and tried to forget about her. That was easier said than done. Though it was true he rarely had time to date, he had tried over the last few years. But none of them could compare to Clara. With her strawberry blonde hair and sparkling green eyes, she possessed an aura that could charm even the toughest grinch. No matter what he tried to do, he couldn't seem to get her out of his mind.

He took a seat between Tucker and Jefferson in the back row as most of the other seats were already filled. The other men must have come straight from the cafeteria.

A few minutes later, the head trainer, Justin, walked in. "Good morning. As you all know, Doug left us suddenly to follow his wife. Though there are only a few games left this season, we didn't want to go into the final games a trainer down, so we put out some feelers, and I'm pleased to say we've found a trainer to take his spot. She comes to us with extensive knowledge and expertise."

She? Mason had been spacing out, but at the mention of the feminine pronoun he sat up straighter. True, Clara probably wasn't the only woman who wanted to be an athletic trainer, but he didn't know very many. Could they have actually hired her?

"She's been working with the University of Texas but is excited to join us now. Though she'll be working mainly with the offensive line, I'm sure all of you will chat with her at one point or another. Please help me welcome Clara Bradford."

Mason gasped and leaned forward as if he'd been punched. Clara was here?

"You okay?" Tucker whispered beside him.

Mason shook his head but didn't even glance toward his friend. His eyes were glued on the door. He saw the shimmery red of her hair before the rest of her appeared. She was a little older but no less beautiful. In fact, if it was possible, he thought she was even prettier than before. Her face was a little more defined, and there was a glow to it that hadn't been there before.

Though she was smaller than Justin and probably every man in the room, she commanded attention. She always had. It had been one of the first things that drew Mason to her. "I'm pleased to meet you all and look forward to working with you the rest of this season."

"I bet a lot of the guys are going to look forward to working with her too," Jefferson said in a hushed whisper.

Mason shot him a glare. He had been so excited to see Clara again that he hadn't even thought about her working with the other men. It would kill him if any of them started seeing her. He could only hope that she wouldn't mix business and pleasure. Or that he could convince her they belonged together before she fell for anyone else.

His gaze traveled back to Clara, and her eyes caught his. She flashed a small smile, sending his heart thudding in his chest. Was she happy to see him? Surprised? Surely, she must have known this was his team. Had she come hoping to run into him?

"Okay, we'll let you get to the rest of your day. Don't hesitate to come to us if you have any questions."

Justin dismissed the group, and Mason stood to head to an offensive line briefing with the rest of his teammates. His eyes, however, stayed on Clara until he was out of the room.

"You have a thing for the new doc already?" Jefferson asked as he elbowed Mason.

"She's not new to me," Mason returned. "Clara is my ex-girlfriend."

Jefferson's eyes widened. "Oh, man, I'm sorry. Did you know she was coming here?"

Mason shook his head. "We haven't spoken in years. I wasn't even sure she had become an athletic trainer, but I guess that question has been answered at least."

"Are you going to be able to work with her?"

That was a very good question. "Are you kidding? This is my second chance. She said we were too different when we broke up after high school, but here we are, on the same team. That can't be a coincidence, right?"

Jefferson smiled. "You know I don't believe in coincidences. God has a plan for everything in our lives, even when we don't understand it at first."

Mason cocked his head at Jefferson. Why did he get the feeling his teammate was talking more about his own life than Mason's? "Well, I don't know what His original plan might have been, but I'll certainly accept her being in my future."

3

CLARA

C lara looked up at the knock on her office door. Mason stood in there, a smile on his face. "Can I come in?"

"Sure," she said, trying to calm the pounding in her chest. She had loved Mason Dixon since her Sophomore year in high school and breaking up with him had been the hardest thing she'd ever done. Probably the stupidest too, but she'd believed her father when he'd said it was for the best. And she'd tried to put him from her mind, but he'd never been far. She'd always considered him "the one that got away" even though she had initiated their breakup, and though she'd dreamed of seeing him again one day, she hadn't actually thought it would come true.

"How are you settling in?" He rubbed one arm and then

the other in a nervous gesture that made her smile. Could he still have feelings for her as well?

"Well, I'm still unpacking as you see." She motioned to the boxes around her. "My apartment is even more of a mess, but I'm liking it so far."

"I could help if you'd like. Practice is over for the day, and I wouldn't mind catching up with you."

"Really?" Clara wanted to say yes. She wanted to spend time with him, but was that a good idea? She had no idea if anyone knew about their past or if there were rules about dating between team members, but surely no one could condemn two friends catching up. "I mean it's pretty boring unpacking boxes, but if you want."

"I want." He offered a crooked smile and opened one of the boxes. "So, what have you been doing for the last six years? Besides becoming an athletic trainer that is."

Clara chuckled and pulled a few of her medical books out of a box. "That's pretty much it. I went to Texas Tech after high school and spent my years learning sports medicine and working with the team. Then I took a job with The University of Texas after graduation. That's where I've been for the last year." She wondered if he was fishing for information about her romantic life, and the thought made her smile. She had dated a few guys in college and almost gotten engaged to one of her father's employees - that was a long story - but none of them had held a candle to Mason, and she doubted he really wanted to hear that information. More likely, he was fishing to see if she was single, and she was curious if he was as well.

"And what made you want to come here? To Southlake, I mean," he asked as he placed books on the shelf beside hers.

"My friend saw the job offer and she knew I'd always wanted to work for a professional team. I didn't think I had a chance, but she persuaded me to apply, and here I am."

He paused for a second and chewed on his bottom lip as if he wanted to ask something but wasn't sure how. "Did you know?"

"Did I know what?" And then she realized what he was asking. "You mean did I know that you played for the Tornadoes?"

"Yeah." It was only one word, but so much emotion existed in that one word.

"I did." Her heart thudded again as a smile curved his lips. "I followed your career, but I didn't think I'd actually ever work on the same team you played for."

"You used to say that was your dream, before…" Mason shrugged as he let the word trail off, but Clara knew what he was thinking. Before she broke up with him. Before she sent him away, heartbroken and confused. Before she had the courage to stand up to her father. Well, she hadn't really done that yet. She'd simply distanced herself, but one day she would.

"Mason, I…" She paused. She wanted to tell him she was sorry, but if she did, he would want to know why and she couldn't tell him. He looked like he might forgive her now, but if he knew the real reason, she doubted he would.

"Ah, Clara, there you are."

Clara jumped at the sound of Justin's voice in the door-way. Heat climbed across her face as if she and Mason had been caught in a compromising position, and she took a step away from him to increase the distance. "Here I am, unpack-ing. What can I do for you, Justin?"

Justin's eyes narrowed as he looked from Clara to Mason and back again. "I need to get some signatures from you for the paperwork. Do you think we could do that now?"

"Sure, Mason was just helping me unpack, but I can finish that later." She glanced at Mason, hoping he would agree and not say anything about their past to Justin. At least not until she knew what the rules were.

"Yeah, I was just helping her get settled, but I need to be going anyway. It was good to see you again, Clara." Mason flashed her a small smile before stepping past Justin and out of the office.

"Again? You two know each other?" Justin asked.

Clara wondered if he was asking merely out of curiosity or for some other reason. "Yeah, Mason and I went to high school together."

"Aha, well, if you'll come with me, we'll get you taken

care of and you can get back to unpacking before the weekend."

Clara nodded and followed Justin, but her mind was still on Mason. Was he happy she was here? She hoped she would have more time to speak with him soon.

4

MASON

"What's with the goofy smile tonight?" Mason's brother, Duke, asked as he dealt the cards for their weekly Friday night poker game. It wasn't every weekend Mason got to join his brother and their friends, but as they had this weekend off, he had the time.

"I don't know what you're talking about," Mason said, trying to wipe off his grin. It was impossible though because every time he thought about Clara's sweet smile, the corners of his lips lifted again.

"Right," Pete said. "You look like a cat who ate a canary." Pete was one of the first people Mason and Duke had met when they moved to Southlake. He owned a local comic book store and though Mason wasn't a huge fan, Duke was. The man had just about everything Batman that existed.

"Well, can't a guy be happy? We made it to the playoffs

again, I've got another chance at a championship ring, what's not to be happy about?" Mason looked at his cards and tried not to sigh. He enjoyed poker, but it seemed he always had the worst luck whenever he played.

"Yeah, but you knew that last week when we met." Duke tossed a chip into the middle to call. "So, what happened today?"

"Fine," Mason said with a sigh as he tossed his own chip in. "We got a new athletic trainer."

"I thought you liked your old trainer. What was his name? Doug?" Pete looked up as he tossed his chip in to call.

"Yeah, I did. Doug was great, but he left when he got married and today we met the new trainer, and she's also great."

"She?" Duke's brow lifted. "Ah, now I understand the smile. She must be pretty. Is my monk of a brother finally ready to move on with his life?" He laid down the first upturned card of the river.

A three of hearts would not help Mason at all, but he tossed in another chip to call. "Hey, I've dated. They just haven't worked out."

"Because you haven't wanted them to work out. You've been hung up on Clara since she broke up with you."

"Wait, who's Clara?" Pete asked as he raised the pot.

"Just his high school sweetheart who dumped him after graduation for no good reason," Duke replied. "Too rich for my blood. I fold."

"Ouch, that sounds rough," Pete said as Duke laid down the next card. An Ace of Hearts. That would help him as he had an Ace in his hand, but it also might help Pete who seemed to have a never-ending string of luck whenever they played. "So, tell us about this new trainer. What's her name?"

Mason bit his lip. He shouldn't have brought this up. It was obvious his brother was still angry at Clara. He probably should be too, but he was still convinced there was more behind their breakup, especially after today. Still, he'd opened up the can of worms; there was no putting the lid back on now. "Clara."

Though it hadn't been noisy before, the silence that fell around the table was deafening. Mason pushed in a few chips before glancing up. His brother's mouth hung open in shock and the look on Pete's face was pure confusion.

"That's a weird coincidence," Pete said slowly as he matched Mason's chips.

"It's not a coincidence." Duke's voice was low and hard. "He's talking about the girl who stomped on his heart."

"It wasn't exactly like that." Mason's defensive wall was up, but he wasn't sure he could really explain to his brother why not. "I told you I thought her father was the reason for her breaking up with me. Anyway, no one said I was dating her again. It was just nice to see her again, and I'm happy that she's doing what she always wanted to do."

That was mostly the truth, but Mason would be lying if he wasn't hoping there was a chance they would date again.

Clara had been his first love, and he was fairly certain, she was his true love. Perhaps now that she was no longer living under her father's roof, she would see that too.

Duke shook his head sadly as he laid down the next river card. "I know you better than that, Mason. You know I'll support you, but I just hope you aren't headed for Heartbreak Road again."

So did Mason. He'd survived their breakup once, but it had done a number on him. He wasn't sure if he'd survive a second time. "Fold," he said, throwing in his cards. The last card hadn't helped him and he just didn't have the energy to bluff. Maybe coming over here tonight hadn't been the best idea.

5

CLARA

C lara watched the city fade behind her as she headed out of Southlake. It was Saturday, and her day off. Though she had started on a Friday, Justin had still given her the weekend to get settled into her apartment and to take some time to visit her best friend from college, Adrienne.

She and Adrienne had met in the dorms at Texas Tech. Clara had somehow managed to snag a coveted single while Adrienne had been sidled with the roommate from Hades. The two girls had met in the hallway one night and traded horror stories. Clara hated living alone, and Adrienne could barely hear herself think over her roommate's music. At the end of the semester, the two had decided to get an apartment together near campus.

Though nearly polar opposites, somehow it worked for

them. Clara ate a healthy breakfast of a protein waffle or eggs every morning while Adrienne had Dr. Pepper and a bag of Doritos. Clara liked enchiladas while Adrienne ate boxed Mac N Cheese for nearly every dinner, and while Clara had been born in a wealthy family, she'd still had to do her own laundry. Adrienne, however, took her clothes to a dry cleaner and then ironed them again when she got them home.

Clara chuckled as that memory surfaced in her mind. She'd come home to find Adrienne ironing a pair of jeans. Jeans!

"What are you doing?" Clara asked as she watched her friend move the iron slowly over the denim.

Adrienne looked up, confusion clouding her blue eyes. "What does it look like I'm doing? I'm ironing."

"I see that, but why are you ironing jeans?" Clara hated ironing and avoided it whenever possible. Still, she'd been known to use an iron when a dress or nice shirt was too wrinkled, but she'd never once seen anyone iron blue jeans.

Adrienne's brow furrowed. "How else am I supposed to get the crease line?"

Clara threw up her hands and laughed. "Jeans aren't supposed to have a crease line. There's a reason they aren't considered work attire. They're supposed to be casual wear."

"But they look so wrong if they don't have the crease."

Clara hadn't won that argument. Even four years later when the girls had gone their separate ways, Adrienne still ironed her jeans. She had learned to use a washer and dryer though and stopped paying for a dry cleaner. Clara supposed she could count that as a win.

Now, Adrienne was married to a man she had met at her job and had two small children. Clara wondered if Adrienne had relaxed her standards with the addition of the kids. It was certainly hard to keep everything pressed and put away with kids in the picture, but somehow Clara could picture Adrienne wandering through the house after the kids were asleep and picking up after them. At least her diet probably hadn't had to change much. Adrienne had always eaten like a kid which was such an anathema compared to her perfection in every other area of her life.

Adrienne's house was just as Clara pictured it. The grass was manicured to perfection and still green though it was January. They probably had the sprinkler system on a timer if Adrienne's husband was as meticulous as she was. A white picket fence surrounded the land, and a wraparound porch completed the look. Clara pulled up to the side of the fence and turned off the car.

As if she had heard the sound of the car, Adrienne popped out of the front door a moment later. She held her youngest on her hip, and the older boy toddled behind her. It had been a few years, but other than wearing a slightly harried expression, Adrienne looked exactly the same with her long blonde hair, blue eyes, and soft smile.

"Clara, I can't believe you're actually here." Adrienne wrapped her in a side hug with her free arm.

"Me either." The two had talked about getting together for years, but it had never seemed to work out between their schedules.

"Come on inside. I was just about to get lunch going for the kids."

Clara grinned. "Let me guess. Mac N Cheese and Dr. Pepper?"

Adrienne laughed. "Please, I've grown up since then. We add hotdogs now."

The interior of the house was exactly what Clara had pictured. Simple and minimal, everything had its place. Clara wished she had that trait, but organized chaos seemed to be more her style. She knew where everything was, but it appeared a cluttered mess to everyone else.

"So, how is the new job?" Adrienne asked as she plunked the little girl in a high chair and opened the fridge to pull out a bottle of milk. She placed it in the bottle warmer and then moved to the stove to stir the pot.

"It's been good. So far."

Adrienne turned around and fixed her with a knowing stare. "Uh oh, I hear hesitation. What does that mean?"

Clara sighed as she sat down in one of the cream-colored barstools. "You remember that ex-boyfriend I told you about?"

Adrienne's brow furrowed as she thought back through the years. "The one who wanted to be a football player?"

"That's the one. Turns out he made it, and now I'm one of

the athletic trainers on his team." Clara's eyes dropped to the marble counter, and she traced a gold thread that ran through it with her fingertip.

"I see." Adrienne opened a cabinet and grabbed a bowl, filling it with Mac N Cheese and setting it before her son. "And is that an issue because you still care about him?" She grabbed the bottle from the warmer and handed it to the little girl.

"I... I don't know. It was such a mess when we broke up, but I honestly never thought I'd see him again." The memory of her father telling her that she had to break it off with Mason tried to enter her mind, but she pushed it away. She would not revisit that right now.

"And have you spoken with him yet?" Adrienne filled another bowl of Mac N Cheese and offered it to Clara who shook her head. She'd never been able to stomach the taste of the powdered cheese sauce herself.

"Yeah, a little. He came into my office to help me unpack. He didn't seem mad, but we were interrupted by my new boss before we really got to talk much. I'm sure I'll have to work with him soon and I have no idea what to say."

"Do you even know if he's still single?" Adrienne raised a brow as she sat in the barstool across from Clara.

Clara hadn't even considered that. Would it be better if he were taken? Worse? She honestly had no idea. "I don't, but I have been following him a little in the news and they've never mentioned a girlfriend or wife."

"Wait." Adrienne set down the spoonful she was about to eat. "You mean you knew he played for this team when you took the job?"

Clara grimaced and the "yes" she squeaked out was much higher than her normal voice. "You have to understand that this was a huge opportunity. These jobs don't come around very often, and I couldn't not apply."

"Uh huh. I hear that, but I kind of feel like you don't get a pass on this one." She picked up the spoon again and pointed it at Clara. "You knew what you were getting yourself into."

And she had. Sort of. She'd known he would be there, but she hadn't been prepared for the barrage of feelings that would hit her when she saw him again. Nor had she been prepared for her breath to catch around him and her heart to beat faster when he was around or when someone mentioned his name. "Yeah, I guess I did."

Clara didn't want to talk about Mason any longer, and the growling of her stomach reminded her that she hadn't had lunch yet either. "Do you have anything I can make a sandwich with? Or a salad?"

"Of course." Adrienne laid out bread, meat, cheese, and vegetables and Clara fixed herself a decent meal.

"So, how about you?" she asked as she sat down again. "How is your job going?" Adrienne had studied social work in college, and the few times they had spoken on the phone over the years, she had always told Clara how stressful it was but how much she loved it.

Adrienne took a sip of her Dr. Pepper and glanced at the two children to make sure they were still good before answering. "Well, I'm just getting back into the swing of things after maternity leave, but it's harder now."

"What do you mean?"

"I mean having kids of my own. It always broke my heart to see children in bad situations and to have to take them away from their parents, but I knew it was for the best. It hurt even worse when I had to reunite them with those parents before they were really ready in some cases, but now that I have Cade and Chrissy, it's so much harder. Every little face I see reminds me of them, and I think about how awful it would be if someone took them away from me."

Clara looked at the two beautiful children as she chewed. That would be hard to take. She wasn't a mother yet herself, but she knew how much these two meant to Adrienne. After swallowing, she posed the question that sat heavy in the air. "Are you going to keep doing it?"

Adrienne sighed and scooped out the last of her Mac N Cheese. "I don't know. David makes good enough money that I don't have to work, but it's always been a part of me, you know?"

Clara did. Adrienne's father had left when she was little, and her mother had raised Adrienne and her little brother all by herself. Unfortunately, her mother's schedule and absence a lot of the time had strained their relationship, and Adrienne had moved out as soon as she was of age. She'd worked hard to provide for herself and her little brother, and though she had spoken with her mother a few times before her death, Clara wasn't sure she had ever really forgiven her.

"Is there something else you could do in the same line? Maybe running a fostering program or working at an adoption agency?" In truth, Clara had no idea what other avenues Adrienne's degree might work for, but it was worth a thought.

"Yeah, maybe. I'm still thinking about it for now."

"Mommy, can we play in the backyard now?" Cade asked from the table.

His cute voice tugged at Clara's heart. If she hadn't broken things off with Mason, would they be married now? Would she have kids of her own? Maybe a little boy who looked like him that he could play football with in the backyard?

Stop! That was not a path she needed to go down. She'd made her decision years ago when she'd allowed her father to convince her that breaking up with Mason was the right thing to do. There was no going back from there. A husband and kids might still be in her future, but they wouldn't be his kids.

"Sure, Cade, as soon as Miss Clara is ready," Adrienne said as she took her bowl to the sink and washed it. That part hadn't changed either. Adrienne had never been one to leave a dish in the sink; she'd always washed them immediately after use. Clara wondered if that stemmed from being on her own so young and probably not having many dishes to spare.

"I'm ready," she said, balling up the paper towel she had made her sandwich on and tossing it in the trash can she spied by the door. Then she grabbed Cade's bowl and took it to Adrienne, knowing her friend would want to wash it too before heading outside.

When the dishes were washed to Adrienne's satisfaction, she grabbed Chrissy and the four headed out back.

A small play structure, complete with swings and a slide, sat in the yard, and Cade took off running toward it before the door was even shut behind them.

"He must enjoy that," Clara said with a laugh.

Adrienne rolled her eyes. "He does. He is all boy, that one, and we haven't been able to get outside much." The day was unusually warm for January, but Clara knew what she meant. It had been cold and rainy most of the last week.

Just then Cade's cry pierced the air. Clara looked to see him sitting on the ground and holding his arm. Though she hadn't seen it happen, she could imagine he must have slipped on the ladder of the slide and scraped his arm.

"Oh dear, can you hold her?" Adrienne asked, holding out Chrissy for Clara to take.

"Actually, where's your First Aid Kit? I'll fix him up. It's what I do, after all."

Adrienne gave quick directions, and Clara hurried into the house and to the bathroom. In the cabinet under the sink had been Adrienne's words. Clara opened the door and found the kit exactly where she'd said it would be. Another point for a neat and orderly house. If only she could keep hers the same. Then she raced back outside to bandage up the boy.

After a few promises that he was okay and a Band-Aid to cover the scratch, Cade happily went back to the play structure. It was amazing how easily kids could bounce back from tears and hurts. Clara watched him and wished that broken hearts in adults were as easy to mend.

6

MASON

Mason smiled as he brushed a strand of hair from Clara's face. Her lips curled into a smile, and she opened her mouth to speak. Instead of sweet words though, the noise that came out of her mouth was an annoying beeping sound. Mason looked around to see where the noise was coming from, but when his gaze came back to Clara, she was gone.

With a sigh, he realized the offensive noise was his alarm clock and his time with Clara had been nothing but a dream. He slapped the snooze button on the alarm and slowly opened his eyes. He hadn't dreamed about Clara in years, yet she'd visited him nightly since Friday. It had to be because she now worked for his team, and though they had yet to have a meaningful face to face conversation, he had managed to score a little time with her Friday evening before Justin had interrupted them.

Justin. The thought of the way the head trainer had looked at Clara sent a wave of repulsion through his body. It wasn't that Justin was a bad guy, but this was Clara. His Clara, and he couldn't imagine her dating Justin. He was much older than her for one thing, and Mason was pretty sure he'd just gone through a messy divorce.

Kicking back the covers, he swung his legs out of bed and sat up, pausing for a moment to let his body adjust to the new position before he stood. So far, it hadn't been awkward working with her, but she had just started and they hadn't been alone for very long. He needed to find time to speak to her about the past before it did get awkward. They had made it to the playoffs again this year, and he certainly didn't need to be distracted with the most important games ahead of them.

He grimaced slightly when he rose to his feet. He'd twisted his ankle or something during practice on Friday, and though he'd iced it over the weekend, it was still tender. Clenching his jaw, he limped to the shower. Perhaps the hot water would help.

The steam and heat from the water relaxed the muscles of his shoulders, but it did nothing for the pain in his ankle. As he toweled off, he knew he would have to wrap his ankle and hope no one noticed. Thankfully, he always kept medical tape in his bathroom for instances like these.

Sitting on the bed, he wrapped the ankle, careful not to put the tape too tight. The last thing he needed was to lose circulation in the foot and cause an even greater injury. With that deed done, he pulled on clothes, grabbed his wallet, and headed toward the training facility.

The sun was just rising as he pulled into the parking lot, sending brilliant oranges and purples across the sky. Mason hated getting up early, but he sure didn't mind getting to see the Texas sunrises. Though he'd only ever lived in Texas, he'd spent time in other states for games and they just couldn't compare to a Texas sunrise or sunset.

After turning the ignition off, he grabbed his bag and headed toward the front entrance. The pain in his ankle appeared to be less with the support of the tape, and he was fairly certain that he wasn't limping. Which turned out to be a good thing because he reached the front door at the same time Clara did. He hadn't even seen her approaching, but he had been a little distracted by the sky.

"Well, well, well," he said with a teasing lilt as he pulled the door open for her. "I guess you can't avoid me now."

Her mouth dropped open in protest. "I haven't been avoiding you."

He raised his brow at her. "Oh really? The only time we spoke on Friday is when I sought you out." He pointed at himself when he emphasized I and then to Clara with the word you.

Her perfect pink lips pulled into a line before she shook

her head. "Well, in case you hadn't noticed, I have been a little busy unpacking and trying to get settled."

"It's because you can't handle my hotness, right? I mean I didn't have these guns back when we dated." He flexed his arms, enjoying the smile that spread across her face.

Clara rolled her eyes and swatted his arm. "Stop it. Don't be ridiculous."

"Ridiculous?" Mason put on his best hurt puppy dog face. "Are you saying I'm not hot? That I've lost it since we dated?"

"No, that's not what I'm saying at all."

"So, you're saying I never had it? I'm so hurt." He let his mouth fall open in mock hurt, but his eyes twinkled to let her know he was kidding.

"No, I…" Her words faltered and her face flushed as she realized he had caught her.

Feeling just a bit sorry for her, he offered a reprieve. "It's good to see you smile again."

"Thanks, you too."

They stood there for a minute, both unsure of what to say next. Thankfully, or not so thankfully - Mason wasn't really sure which - Justin interrupted their moment. Again. This man was turning out to have the worst timing in history as far as Mason was concerned.

"Ah, good, Clara, there you are. I've got the schedule for today, and I wanted to discuss game procedures since this Sunday will be a game day."

Clara nodded, her demeanor back to all business. "Guess I'll see you later," she said to Mason before following Justin down the hall.

Mason watched her go, unable to keep his eyes from her and the way Justin looked at her or the way his hand touched her lower back as he led her down the hall. Mason knew the man was looking for comfort, but he could only hope that Justin wouldn't find that comfort in Clara's arms.

Pushing the door to the locker room open, he entered and dropped his bag on the bench. A moment later the door opened again, and Blaine strode into the room.

"I was looking for you. Coach wants to see you."

"Me? What for?" All kinds of traitorous thoughts raced through Mason's head. Had they found out about his former relationship with Clara? Was he in trouble for talking to her? Had the coach seen his injury on Friday? Was he in trouble for not reporting it?

Blaine shook his head. "I don't know. He just asked me to find you and send you his way. I'd suggest you don't keep him waiting though. You know how he gets the week before games."

"Right." Coach had a tendency to be a little more high strung and laser-focused the week leading up to a game, and Mason knew better than to keep him waiting. He finished stowing his stuff in the locker and then headed to face the music. Whatever it was.

The anxiety only grew the closer he got to the coach's

office. Before knocking, he took a deep breath and tried to calm his racing heart. It would do no good to enter looking guilty before he knew what the meeting was even about.

"Come in," the coach's deep voice came from the other side of the door.

Mason pushed the door open and hoped he looked more confident than he felt. "You asked for me, Coach?"

"I did. Have a seat." Coach pointed at the chair opposite his desk. "I watched the tape from practice on Friday."

Mason's heart sank as he sat in the chair. This was about his injury then. He wasn't sure if that was the better of the two options or not. "Coach, I can explain…"

Coach held up his hand and fixed Mason with a silencing glare. "How bad is it, Dixon?"

"It's not bad, Coach, really. I landed awkwardly on it, but I iced it all weekend. It's much better today."

Mason tried not to squirm under the coach's penetrating stare. The man's gaze was like an intimidating lie detector. "Okay, well, I want you to see the new athletic trainer today. Have it looked at and taped up, and take it easy on that foot. We need you for Sunday's game."

"Yes, sir." Relief flooded Mason as he stood. Yes, he might have to meet with Clara, but he was pretty sure he had just dodged a bullet in there.

He returned to the locker room and changed into his practice gear before heading to find Clara.

She was staring down at her desk when he knocked on

the door. He must have startled her because her small jump sent the papers on her desk flying to the floor. Mason rushed over to help her pick them up.

"Sorry, I didn't mean to startle you."

"No, it's fine. I was just focused and not expecting anyone for another hour."

They each grabbed for the papers, their hands touching as they reached for the same one at the same time. His eyes locked with hers and memories from their time together flooded him. He remembered the first time he held her hand. He had thought at the time that he'd been so suave - pretending to yawn and then placing the hand he covered his mouth with on top of hers. She had smiled but said nothing, and he'd fallen even harder for her.

He let go first, hoping to sever the memories as well as the connection he was feeling right now. "Sorry." He picked up the rest of the papers that were out of her reach and placed them on her desk.

"It's okay." She stood after gathering her stack of papers. "What are you doing here?"

Mason shrugged. "Coach sent me to see you before practice. I twisted my ankle last Friday, and he wanted it checked out and taped up." He pointed down at his foot. "However, I did that this morning."

She raised an eyebrow at him and pointed to the bed that sat in her office. "Well, if Coach wants me to take a look at it, you better sit down and let me see it."

Mason took a deep breath as he walked to the bed. He hoped Clara wouldn't be able to see anything wrong. There was no way he was missing Sunday's game.

After sitting, he untied his shoe and stretched his leg out.

She started at his knee, her fingers probing down his leg. He tried not to flinch at her touch. It certainly didn't hurt, but it was igniting things in his body that he hadn't felt for years.

He was so focused on the memories that he had stopped paying attention to where her fingers were until she pressed on something that sent a pain up his leg and forced him to jump and cry out in pain. Her eyes flicked to his, brimming with concern.

"That hurt?"

"Just a little." He clenched his jaw to keep from showing her how much. "I probably just need to ice it more."

"Mason, I don't think you should be running on this ankle. I'm not sure this is a twisted ankle or even a strain or sprain. In fact, I'd like to get an MRI. I'm afraid you've injured your Achilles or you might be developing tendonitis in it."

"What? No. I'm too young for that." There was no way he was getting an MRI. He knew what the recommendation for Achilles tendonitis was - rest - and there was no way he was not playing. "It's a simple sprain, that's all. Look, I'll take it easy today and soak it more tonight. After Sunday's game, we'll have another week off. That will give it plenty of time to heal."

Clara was not convinced. That was evident by her pursed lips and folded arms, but he knew she wouldn't fight him on it. At least, not yet. He'd just have to tell the offensive line coach he needed to play conservatively and let his ankle heal. As long as it didn't get worse, he didn't think Clara would rat him out. At least he hoped not.

CLARA

Clara kept an eye on Mason during practice. He didn't appear to be favoring the ankle, but she also knew he was a master of disguising injuries. She had seen it first hand in high school when he'd strained his shoulder and played anyway because a scout was coming. Thankfully, he'd been able to catch with the other hand and he hadn't done further damage to his shoulder, but this ankle injury was a whole other matter. If it truly was Achilles tendonitis like she suspected, continuing to play on it could lead to a rupture.

"You watch any harder and you might stare a hole in the guy," Davis said, coming up beside her. Davis was one of the other trainers, and she liked him. He seemed approachable and down to earth and the wedding band on his hand assured her he wouldn't be flirting with her unlike some of the other men who had approached her over the last few days.

She folded her arms across her chest. "I'm worried about Mason. He came in Monday with a slight limp, and while he swore to give it some rest, it sure doesn't look like he's resting it to me."

"Did you examine him?"

"As much as I could." She shrugged and blew out an exasperated breath. "I think it's Achilles Tendonitis, but he refuses to get an MRI to verify."

Davis let out a low whistle. "Well, I can see why. If that's what it is, it would take him out of the game this weekend and maybe the rest of the play-off games if they win."

"I know, but wouldn't that be better than it rupturing?" She bit her lip, unsure of what to do. On one hand, she wasn't one hundred percent sure, and she didn't want to jeopardize his playing time if she was wrong. She also didn't want to be responsible for a worse injury if she was right.

"You can't make him listen to you though. Massage it after every practice, make sure he's icing it and resting it at home, and tell Justin if you're really worried. That's about all you can do."

Clara nodded. That was sound advice, and she had been following the first step since she found out about it. Perhaps, she could offer to make him dinner tonight to make sure he was resting it properly at home.

"How is the ankle feeling?" she asked as Mason climbed up on her table that afternoon after practice.

"Are you asking as my trainer or my friend?" he asked with a hesitant smile.

"Both. I wouldn't be doing my professional duty if I didn't check up on you, but as your friend, I'm worried you're pushing it." She unlaced his shoe and pulled it off, watching his face for any indication of pain.

"I really think it's getting better. Felt no pain today."

Clara pulled his sock down and carefully unwound the tape. "It's still swollen though, Mason. I'm not sure you're giving it enough rest."

"Well, I try to put it up at night when I get home, but I do still have things to do after practice. You know eating, cleaning, etc." He flashed her a charming smile as if that made it all better.

"Yes, and speaking of which, how about I make you dinner tonight? That way you can totally put your foot up and ice it, and I'll feel a little better about how much you've been running on it." She threw the question out there but kept her eyes on his ankle as her fingers massaged the tissue around the tendon.

"You want to make me dinner? To rest my foot?" She could hear the disbelief and the note of teasing in his voice.

"I do. Plus, it would give us some time to catch up. We

haven't really gotten to talk much." She really did want to know how the last few years had been for him, whether he was dating anyone, if he still cared about her.

"Are you sure that's allowed? I think Justin might have his sights set on you."

"Ew." She scrunched her nose and stopped massaging his ankle to look at him. "He's got to be close to forty, right?" Realizing she had spoken the words aloud, she quickly scanned the room to make sure Justin wasn't around. She liked him. As a boss. But there was nothing beyond that. Not for her at least.

Mason chuckled and flashed her a wink. "Yeah, I think he might be just over forty and recently divorced. Hot commodity on the market. You might want to snatch him up before someone else does."

Clara swatted his leg. "No thank you. I don't date my bosses anyway. That never works out well."

Mason's brow lifted in curiosity. "Tried that once, did you?"

She flashed a small smile in return, but she didn't tell him about the guy her father had most recently pushed on her. He hadn't really been her boss, at least not her direct boss. No, he'd been bigger than that - the assistant head of the Athletics Department at the University of Texas, and she still hadn't broken up with him directly. She figured he had gotten the hint when she stopped returning his calls and moved, but she still felt a little badly for the way she had ghosted him.

However, Mason did not need to know about that, so she deflected his comment and changed the subject. "Anyway, dinner?"

Though she didn't look at him, she could feel his gaze raking over her, trying to figure out what she wasn't saying. He'd always been good at reading her, but she hoped he wasn't doing so now. "Okay, dinner sounds good."

"Good." She finished massaging his ankle and handed him some Ibuprofen and her business card. "Take these, get cleaned up, and then ice that ankle. Text me your address, and I'll be there around seven."

Mason popped the ibuprofen and pocketed her card. "Sounds good. I'll see you then." He put his sock and shoe back on, flashed her a little wave, and sauntered out of her office.

Clara collapsed into her chair and dropped her head in her hands. She hoped she hadn't just made a huge mistake.

8
MASON

Mason felt strange sitting on his couch and waiting for Clara to show up. He certainly didn't mind propping his ankle up; he'd had to work hard to keep from showing the pain on his face when she'd been massaging it, but sitting around was not his style.

His phone chimed, letting him know a text message had arrived, and a moment later, a knock sounded at his door. He smiled as he cleared the message from Clara letting him know she had arrived. While he appreciated her thoughtfulness, the text was unnecessary.

"I thought I told you to rest that ankle," she said when he opened the door.

Mason chuckled and shook his head as he stepped back to let her enter. "I was resting it until someone knocked on my door. As you don't have a key, and I assume you haven't gained the ability to walk through walls, I figured I would get up long enough to let you in."

A light pink color spread across her cheeks. "Oh, I guess that is true. Well, now that I'm here, I'd like you to get back to relaxing while I get this set up." She nodded toward the large container in her arms.

"Are you cooking here or is it all prepared in that thing?" He indicated her bundle, a smile pulling at the corners of his lips. "I'm just asking because I'd like to know where to sit to rest up."

Clara shot him a narrowed gaze, but the corners of her lips twitched. "You can set up wherever you want to eat. It's all prepared; I just have to dish it out."

"Fine, let me show you the dining room." Mason led the way out of the living room and to his spacious kitchen and dining area. Though his ankle was still throbbing, he made sure to walk evenly on it. Letting Clara know he was still in pain was not an option.

"You've got a nice place here," Clara said from behind him. "I'm glad to see you've done so well."

His house was larger than the one he'd grown up in, but it was no mansion. Clara was used to a much nicer place with her father's money, but her words still made him smile. He'd often wondered if her money had been part of the issue that drove them apart. She'd never seemed to let it when they'd dated, but perhaps her father had convinced her it would one day. Having her compliment his house helped ease those fears a little.

"Thank you. It's modest, but I also sent a large part of my signing bonus to my parents for them to make improvements on their house. Are you going to need anything?"

"Just plates, utensils, and cups, but I can find them on my own. You take a seat." She pointed to the table and then set her contraption on the bar. "Do you have an ice pack? I'd like you to ice it while I get set up."

"There should be a cold one in the freezer. I always have a few on hand." He sat down in one of the chairs, propping his ankle up in another as she crossed to the stainless-steel freezer and opened the door.

After pulling out an ice pack, she wrapped it in a paper towel to keep the chill from burning his skin and then placed it on his ankle. Mason tried to calm his racing heart as her fingers touched his skin. It had been like this every day this week. He knew there was nothing going on between them right now, but every time he was around her, his pulse raced.

"That okay?"

He nodded, his throat constricting at the tenderness he saw in her eyes. Why did she have such an effect on him? Especially after the way she broke things off with him. He should be mad. He should hate her, but he couldn't do it.

She returned to the bar and opened her contraption, pulling out a large bowl that he assumed held the spaghetti as well as a smaller bowl and a rectangular pan. Then she turned and began opening his cabinets, pulling out plates, forks, and cups. She looked so at home in his kitchen that he found himself imagining her there every day. What would it be like to come home to a cooked meal instead of take out or whatever he grabbed on his way home?

Clara scooped out spaghetti onto each plate. Then she opened the smaller bowl and added salad beside the noodles. Finally, she pulled a piece of garlic bread from the rectangular container and placed one on each plate. With a flourish like a well-trained waitress, she delivered a plate to him and set another one down for herself.

"This looks delicious, Clara," Mason said as his stomach rumbled. The smell of the garlic and spices was enticing and sent his mouth watering. Pasta was not normally on his diet during game season, but he figured one night wouldn't hurt, and he had run hard today. That much was evident from the throbbing in his ankle.

"It should be. It's my mother's recipe, the one you loved in high school," Clara said with a smile.

Memories of dinners spent at the Bradford's flooded Mason's mind, and the need to know what really happened burned once again in his chest. "I always loved Italian night at your house." Clara's mother had been Italian though Clara resembled her English father more.

"Yeah, they were good." Clara's voice was soft with wistfulness, and though Mason wanted to probe the past, he didn't want to ruin the moment.

"Well, to a nice dinner between old friends," Mason said, lifting his glass.

"I'll drink to that." Clara lifted her own glass and clinked it against his.

The conversation stalled as they ate, each seemingly lost in their own worlds. Though he tried not to stare, Mason's eyes flicked to Clara several times throughout the meal. How many times had he dreamed about meals like this with her? Too many to count, and a part of him still didn't believe it was real.

"Clara, what really happened between us?" he asked, breaking the silence.

Her expression tightened, and he immediately wished he could take the question back. "It was a long time ago, Mason. Can't we just let it go?"

"I just need to know, Clara. You said it was because we were too different, but look at us now." He motioned with his hands to the table. "We're having dinner together, we work for the same team, we like the same food; what makes us so different? Was it just because I was poor?"

Her mouth dropped open as if he'd slapped her. "Mason, no, I would never break up with anyone simply because they had less money than I did."

"Then, why, Clara?" He was pushing the subject and he knew it, but he couldn't seem to stop himself. The need to know the real reason burned within him like an eternal flame.

"I can't..." She shook her head, her words trailing off.

Anger flared up inside Mason. "You can't? Or you won't?"

"Mason, you don't understand."

"You're right. I don't understand. You know what? I've lost my appetite and I feel like going to bed." He pushed his chair back and stood, but his ankle wasn't prepared for the weight, and he grimaced before grabbing on to the table top.

"Your ankle isn't better, is it?" Clara's voice was low and serious. "Mason, if it's not getting better, you have to skip Sunday's game and let it rest."

Mason shook his head and placed the rest of his weight on his ankle, ignoring the pain licking up his calf. "You know what, Clara? You might be my trainer, but you lost the right to tell me what to do years ago. I'm playing on Sunday, and there's nothing you can do about it."

With that he whirled away from her and headed upstairs. She could see herself out, and he could lock the door later.

9

CLARA

Clara watched Mason limp up the stairs and bit her lip. That hadn't gone the way she'd wanted it to at all. Perhaps she should have just told him the truth, but she knew the moment she did, his view of her would change forever. And she wasn't ready for that yet.

Even worse, she'd upset him, causing him to aggravate his injury. Every bone in her body screamed that he shouldn't play on Sunday, but he wasn't going to listen to her. Did she tell Justin then? If she did and Mason was benched, he might never forgive her. But if she didn't and he got injured, could she forgive herself?

"Lord, I need some advice," she whispered softly as she gathered up the dishes. Mason had made it clear he wanted her gone, but she wasn't about to leave him with a sink full of dirty dishes. Especially when it had been her idea to cook for him.

When the dishes were washed, she gathered her own supplies and packed them back in her carrying case. With a final glance up the silent stairs, she sighed and headed back to her car.

As soon as she slid into the seat and the door closed behind her, she pulled out her phone. Surprised to see three missed calls, she swiped the screen, shaking her head when Joel's name popped up. Was the man so dense that he didn't realize her lack of communication was her breaking things off? Sure, it was a little cowardly, but it also saved her from having to deal with her father which was the most important thing.

Ignoring Joel's calls, she dialed Adrienne instead, hoping she wasn't interrupting dinner or some other family time.

"Hey, girl, what's up?" Adrienne's chipper voice said when the line stopped ringing.

"I need advice." Clara laid out the night and the additional information about Mason's injury and waited.

"Let me ask you a question," Adrienne said after a long pause. "Do you still love him?"

"What?" Clara hadn't mentioned anything about her feelings for Mason nor had that been part of her question. Besides, what did it have to do with his treatment?

"You heard me. Do you still love him?" Adrienne said each word slowly as if that might help Clara understand the question. "The way I see it is *that* is the most important question. If you love him and want a second chance with him, then tell him about your father. Explain to him why you broke up with him. Otherwise, it's always going to be a bone of contention between the two of you. If you don't love him, then it doesn't matter and you're worrying about it for nothing. If this were any other player that you didn't have a history with, would you tell your head trainer?"

Clara sighed. "Yeah, I probably would. Football players are stubborn and whether Justin does anything about it or not, at least I'll have put my two cents in, but Mason isn't just some normal player."

"Exactly, which is why you need to be honest with yourself and decide if you still love him."

Clara knew Adrienne was right, but sometimes she hated the fact that her friend could put the answer out so plainly and yet avoid the question entirely. She'd wanted advice from her friend, but instead all she had was an even bigger question to consider.

"Thanks, A. I guess I've got some soul searching to do."

"I'm always here when you need some honesty," Adrienne said with a laugh. "Oops, gotta run. Baby needs a bath. Tell me how it goes."

The phone went dead in Clara's ear and she placed it on the dashboard holder before backing out of Mason's driveway.

Did she love him? That was a very good question. She

cared about him for sure, and she had loved him once, but that had been years ago. Yet, if she were honest with herself, part of why his injury bothered her so much was because she was worried about him. More worried than she would be about a normal player.

The question still plagued her half an hour later as she pulled into the parking lot of her apartment complex, and she had a feeling it wouldn't get resolved any time soon.

CLARA STOOD BEFORE JUSTIN'S DESK THE NEXT MORNING with butterflies in her stomach. She had tossed and turned most of the night, and while she still wasn't sure of her feelings for Mason, she was sure that telling Justin of his injury was the right thing. Once he knew, the weight of guilt could be lifted from her shoulders as the decision of whether Mason could play or not would be on Justin and not her.

"Clara, what can I do for you this morning?" Justin smiled as he looked up at her.

"I wanted to talk to you about Mason Dixon," she said softly. Though she'd made up her mind, it didn't make the words any easier to say.

"Is there a problem?" Justin stood and walked around his desk before leaning against it. Clara wanted to take a step back away from him, but she held her ground.

"Maybe." She swallowed hard, summoning the courage to continue. "He hurt his ankle last Friday in practice and the coach sent him to see me. I examined him, and I think it might be Achilles Tendonitis, but he won't go in for an MRI. He's been icing it, but it's still bothering him, and I'm worried about him playing on Sunday."

Justin folded his arms across his chest and regarded her. "What does Mason say?"

"That it's just a strain. He says he's putting it up at night and icing it and that he's fine to play."

"Well, then I think there's your answer."

Clara's mouth dropped open in surprise. "You aren't even going to examine him to be sure?"

"Look, Clara, we do our job to the best of our abilities. We examine the athletes and give them our suggestions, but these are grown men. They're going to do what they think is best for themselves and for their careers. I appreciate your concern, but I have to ask one thing. Is there more perhaps to this concern? Maybe the fact that you knew him from high school." He lifted an eyebrow as he posed the question.

Clara felt herself bristle. Was Justin asking out of curiosity's sake or for some other reason? "I've known Mason for a long time, but my concern is for his health. Nothing more."

Justin stared at her a moment longer as if gauging her sincerity before nodding. "Well, you've done your duty then. I'll note your concerns about his injury, but unless something changes my mind during practice today, he'll be playing on Sunday."

"Very good, sir." Clara wasn't happy with the decision, but she had made her concerns known. All she could do now was continue to work with him and pray that God protected him.

10

MASON

Mason dragged his feet as he walked down the hall to Clara's office. He didn't want to meet with her today. Not after last night's dinner, but not meeting with her would get back to coach which would put him in more trouble. So, he'd get in, get wrapped up, and get out. No focusing on her or the past. Just business.

"Hey," she looked up as he knocked on her door. She stood, but there was a look of uncertainty on her face. "About last night..."

He held up his hand. "Forget it. You were right. There's no need to rehash the past. We aren't dating. You're my trainer, nothing more."

A look of hurt flashed across her eyes, but Mason ignored it. He needed to focus on the game and not on Clara. Crossing to the bed, he sat down and propped up his ankle.

"Right," she said, blinking. "Did you put it up last night after I left at least?"

"Of course I did, and there's still nothing to worry about. I just stood up too fast last night is all."

Clara pursed her lips and shook her head as she began examining his ankle. "You know that's not true. I'm really worried about you playing Sunday, but Justin said the decision was yours."

Mason tensed. "You told Justin?"

Clara paused and bit her lip. She evidently hadn't meant to let that slip. "I had to, Mason. You may not like my advice, but I would have told him if it were any other player."

Mason blew out a disgusted breath. "I can't believe you, Clara. I'm not just any other player. I thought…" He shut his mouth. There was no way he was telling her that he'd thought they would have a second chance now. She could have ruined his career.

"You thought what?"

"Nothing. It doesn't matter. Examine me, tape me up, and let me get out there. I've got a final practice to get through before game day on Sunday."

The hurt deepened on her face, etching out tiny lines in her forehead and near her eyes, but she said nothing more. After examining the ankle, she wrapped it in tape and handed him some ibuprofen. "Be sure to take these, and I'll see you after practice for a massage."

"You know what? I think I'll skip the after-practice

massage," Mason said as he took the pills. "I've got a date with the hot tub tonight which should do the trick."

Clara looked like she wanted to argue, but she merely nodded and returned to her desk.

Mason thought he would feel better about his victory. After all, he had basically won that sparring match, so why did he feel even worse? The image of the hurt brimming in Clara's eyes refused to leave his mind. A night out. That's what he needed tonight.

He'd do his hot tub soak, shower, and then see if Duke was up for some company. With his night planned, he forced a smile to his face and jogged out onto the field.

"SO, LAST WEEK YOU WERE GUSHING ABOUT HER AND NOW you don't like her?" Duke asked, dipping his French fry in ketchup before shoving it in his mouth. Mason had managed to convince Duke to postpone the regular Friday night poker game and come out to dinner with him since he would be boarding a plane tomorrow and heading to the hotel they'd stay in before the playoff game on Sunday.

"She could have damaged my career, Duke. Over nothing, just a little strain." He'd told himself it was nothing so often that he was almost believing it.

Duke took a sip of his coke and then scratched the side of his face. "I don't understand. If it's just a strain, how could that have damaged your career? You've played with strains before, right?"

Mason realized his mistake and tried to backpedal. "Yeah, but she thinks it's something more. If Justin had told the coach, they might have benched me until it was checked out, and there is no way I'm missing Sunday's game." He took a bite of his grilled chicken and dropped his gaze to his plate, hoping Duke wouldn't press the issue.

"And what does she think it is?"

No such luck. "Achilles Tendonitis, but she's wrong."

Duke set down his burger and leaned forward. "And what if she isn't wrong? What can happen?"

Mason swallowed. He hadn't wanted to think about it, but ever since Clara had mentioned it, he'd spent a fair amount of time googling the injury. "If she's right, and I continue to play on it, there is an increased chance of a tear or a rupture."

"A rupture?" The words exploded from Duke's mouth, turning a few nearby heads their direction. He lowered his voice and leaned forward. "Meaning you couldn't walk?"

Mason used his fork to move his broccoli around on his plate. He really wanted a burger and fries like Duke, but the spaghetti from a few days ago was still sitting heavy in his stomach. He needed to eat clean until the game now to be in his best condition. He speared a broccoli and dipped it in some of the teriyaki sauce that had pooled off his chicken. Anything to keep his gaze from the fiery eyes of his brother. "The risk is small, Duke, and if something happens, there are surgeries now that could fix me up over the summer. I just need to get through the play-off games. Then I can rest it."

"Why?" Duke leaned back and crossed his arms. "Why is it so important you win another championship game? You won last year. You've shown me the ring a dozen times to prove it, so why do you have to win again?"

"Because..." Mason paused. He didn't really have a good reason. Because he needed to prove he could? Why? That had been his fueling mantra, but it had existed because he'd needed to prove to Clara they belonged together. He'd become a professional to prove to her father he was good enough and to make sure he had the kind of money she was used to. He'd pushed himself hard last year to prove he was the best so that if he ever had a second chance, she'd have no reason to say no. But none of that had mattered. His present hadn't changed anything because she still wouldn't tell him about the past.

"I don't know," Mason said. "It's just part of the game. It's what we work all year for, you know?"

"I do know," Duke said with a tone that showed he did understand even if his job was different. "I work hard pitching presentations and sometimes I work on them for months, but we don't get the client. However, not getting a client isn't the end of the world. There are always more clients. Just like there will always be more games, as long as you take care of yourself."

Duke's words made sense, and deep down, Mason knew

it was more than a strain. Or maybe it was a strain, but a pretty bad one. A part of him even knew that Clara was probably right and he shouldn't play in Sunday's game, but he also knew he wouldn't sit it out. He couldn't. He needed to be right. He just no longer knew why.

CLARA

The flurry of nerves in her stomach was almost comforting. Clara couldn't believe that she was going to be on the field during a professional football game. And not just any game. A playoff game. This was more than she'd ever dreamed, but while she was excited, she was also concerned about Mason.

After their failed dinner, the next session with him had been uncomfortable to say the least. He'd brushed off her concerns and then stated it was just work. As if she meant nothing to him. That had certainly stung. Then he'd refused her offer to massage his ankle after practice. He'd promised to rest it, and he hadn't seemed worse, but she wasn't confident he was getting better either which was why she'd gone to Justin. Something she never should have let slip to Mason, especially since Justin had seen no need to examine him. She could understand Mason's hurt, but why couldn't he understand that she was not only just doing her job but that she pushed because she cared about him?

She wanted to believe that he knew what he was doing, but what if he was wrong? What if he went out there today and ruptured it? She hadn't given him any cortisone injections, but what if one of the other trainers had? She'd documented her thoughts on the injury, but what if they hadn't checked or Mason had convinced them she was wrong? Suddenly, she wasn't sure the anti-inflammatories she had brought for him were the best idea. Maybe she should ask Justin if he'd received anything else.

Clara looked over to Justin, but he was engaged in what appeared to be a serious discussion with one of the coaches. Now was definitely not the time. Besides, he hadn't taken her concern seriously when she'd approached him earlier in the week. Why would he now?

"So, are you excited?" a voice to her right asked.

She turned to see Davis, her fellow offensive trainer, setting up supplies at his makeshift station. It was weird traveling and not having her office to attend to the players in, but at least she didn't appear to be setting up her station wrong. It looked like Davis's.

"I am. A little nervous though."

"Ah, you'll be fine. The guys love you." Davis smiled

and leaned forward, lowering his voice as if sharing a secret. "Although I think they really just enjoy having a woman around."

Clara felt her face flush. She had wondered the same thing. Though no one had blatantly hit on her, she'd felt lingering stares and smoldering glances from several of the players. She wondered if they knew of her former relationship with Mason and if they would still be interested in her if they did.

"Thank you. How much action do we typically see in a game? I mean, is it just shots and taping and maybe some stretching?"

Davis shrugged and pulled more supplies out of his box. "It depends on the game, but yeah, if we're lucky, that's all it is."

Just then, the noise increased tenfold as the players began filing in for pre-game preparations. It was a steady stream of cortisone shots, medical tape, and ibuprofen. At least until Mason came in.

"How's the ankle feeling today?" Though she tried, she could not keep the concern out of her voice.

"It's fine. Never better." There was a clipped bravado to his voice that she wasn't used to hearing and she wondered if it was for her benefit or the other players'?

"Right, well, I'm going to check it anyway." She patted the popup cot they had set up. Things had been tense between them, but Achilles Tendonitis, if that's what he had, was nothing to play around with. Unfortunately, he still hadn't let her order any tests. In fact, he had barely spoken to her on the flight over, at the hotel the day before, or on the ride to the stadium.

Her fingers pressed the area around his tendon. The swelling appeared to be less, but did that really mean it was healing? "The swelling does feel like it's down a little."

"I feel fine, Clara. Really."

She paused her examination to look at him. He did seem more relaxed. She didn't see the clenched jaw she had seen over the last few days, and his eyes were focused and held her gaze. Maybe the hot tub had been good for him.

She sighed, wishing they could patch their relationship the same way she could patch his ankle. "Okay, I'm going on the record that I still think it's too soon, but I'll get you wrapped up."

Grabbing the medical tape, she wrapped his ankle and then added a few more times around just for good measure.

"Please be careful," she said as he scooted off the table.

His gaze held hers for a moment, and all the emotions from their previous relationship flooded her. Though they were not alone, the world around them seemed to fade, and she could hear the pounding of her heart in her head. For a moment, the distrust and anger was gone from his eyes, and she wondered if he was feeling the same thing she was - this desire to try again.

"I will," he said and then he was gone.

Clara leaned against the table and sighed as she waited for the next player. She wished she felt better about Mason playing.

MASON

Mason breathed a sigh of relief as he left Clara's table. Though he did feel a lot better, he was still surprised he'd managed to convince her he was fine. She'd been such a stickler, even taking his condition to Justin, that he'd expected a little more pushback. Perhaps she had taken his last words to heart. Besides, he had taken it easier this week which had helped with his ankle. Still, he knew that if she was right, or even if it were a more severe strain than he thought, that his tendon needed more than one good week. But this was a play-off game, and there was no way he was missing it.

With a few minutes to kill before warm up, he decided to give his parents a call. It was tradition, a call before every game so his father could urge him to play his best and his mother could voice her worry over him. Duke had already done his fair share Friday night when they'd had dinner. He appreciated their interest, but sometimes he did wish they would just wish him luck instead of heap extra stress on him.

"Hey, son, you ready to take home the Most Valuable Player trophy today?" his father asked as soon as he answered the phone. Not hello. Not how are you, but are you going to be the best?

Mason ran a hand across the back of his neck as he stifled a sigh. "I'll do my best, Dad, but there are a lot of good players on the team, and it depends on the defense." This was his response every time his father asked this. Would he like to be named MVP of a game? Sure, but he wasn't holding his breath. A lot of factors went into that nomination.

First, they needed to win which was never a given. Second, he needed to have the most receptions leading to touchdowns. The other two receivers were just as good as he was, and if they got the ball more or evaded the defense better, they might be given the nomination as well. There was also Blaine - quarterbacks were given the honor more often than other players - and Tucker, who was a phenomenal running back and might score more touchdowns, to consider. Then there was the occasional time a defensive player made some great turnovers that led to touchdowns and took the title. Needless to say, him winning the title was more of a crap shoot than anything.

"I know you can do it, son. It will just take a little extra effort on your part. Run a little faster, make sure you hold on to the ball, get away from the defenders."

Yes, it sounded so easy when his father said it like that. Unfortunately, his father was an armchair quarterback who had never played football a day in his life. That meant he was great at doling out advice, but he had no idea how much work actually went into said advice.

"Yeah, I'll do my best, Dad." Just like I always do, he added to himself.

"Please be careful, honey," his mother spoke up. "I had a dream last night that you took a hard hit, and I woke up sweaty and scared this morning. Tell me that you'll try not to get hit."

"It's football, honey, getting hit is part of the game," his father cut in before Mason could say a word.

"Dad's right, Mom. Getting hit is unavoidable, but I'm sure it was just a dream. Remember it looks worse on TV than it usually is."

"I know. I just want you to be safe. We barely got to see you over Christmas, and we'd like for you to be able to travel when the season ends and spend more time with us."

"I will, Mom. I promise." He didn't tell her that the reason he'd cut his stay short over Christmas was that he'd been afraid to run into Clara. Nor had he told his parents that Clara now not only lived in the same city he did but worked for the Tornadoes. At least he had no reason to avoid going home now.

The locker room door opened, and Mason quickly ended the call after promising to call them again soon. He had just stowed the phone back in his bag when Blaine and Tucker rounded the corner.

"What ya doing there, Dixon?" Blaine asked with a teasing grin.

"You have a girlfriend you haven't told us about?" Tucker added.

Mason shook his head and hoped the heat he felt creeping up his neck didn't make it to his face. "Nah, just checking messages. No time for a woman right now. I don't know how you two do it."

"Best thing that's ever happened to me," Tucker said. He elbowed Blaine, "Wouldn't you agree?"

"Absolutely. A good woman makes it all worth it."

Mason could agree with them there. He'd felt that way when he and Clara were together. In fact, he'd thought they would marry - he'd even planned out how he would ask her - but before he ever got the chance, she'd broken up with him and without much of an explanation. If she could do that to him, then couldn't any woman? Maybe he was just a bad judge of character.

He thought of the final words Clara had said to him. "Please be careful." He wondered if her concern was merely for his injury or if she still felt for him as well. The look in her eyes made him think she might still have feelings, but their interactions this week certainly hadn't supported that.

He shook his head. Now was not the time to think about that.

"Yeah, well, maybe I'll find one of those someday."

Blaine smiled and clapped him on the shoulder. "You will. Don't worry. God has a plan for you too, but right now, we better get on the field and warm up."

Mason followed Blaine and Tucker out onto the field. He wished he had the faith in God that Blaine did, but ever since Clara had broken his heart, he just hadn't been able to get back to church. Maybe that's what God was waiting for though. Maybe He was waiting for Mason to come back to Him before He sent a partner. He'd go back then. As soon as the season ended and he had the time.

The view as they stepped out onto the field took Clara's breath away. The field itself couldn't be much larger than college fields, but the stands were packed which made it feel so much bigger.

"Pretty impressive, isn't it?" Justin said from behind her.

Clara forced a smile and took a small step to her left. She liked Justin, as a boss, but he'd been acting as if he were going to ask her out since she'd started, and she wanted none of that. Not only was he probably ten years her senior, but he reeked of a recent divorce. She had no desire to be anybody's rebound girl, even if her heart hadn't still been attached to Mason.

"Yeah, it is."

His eyes raked over her for a moment, and then he jerked his head to the right. "We set up over here."

She followed him to a shaded area where a single table and several chairs were set up near a pop-up medical tent. They were a fairly new addition to the pro football arena to allow players privacy if they were injured on the field. Clara wasn't sure how she felt about them. On one hand, she agreed that players deserved their privacy, but on the other hand, she also knew that sometimes players were pressured to get a shot and keep playing when their injury might be much more serious.

Several feet from the table and chairs, players were stretching and tossing balls back and forth to each other. Her eyes found Mason, and she couldn't help but admire how good he looked in the tight pants. Though she'd seen him in uniform in high school - and he had looked good then - he had definitely filled out and put on some muscle since then.

He'd always had broad shoulders, but the pads made his waist look even trimmer. She could see his muscles flex as he ran to catch a ball, and she held her breath hoping that there would be no grimace of pain. Relief flooded her when he appeared to be okay.

Before she knew it, the game was beginning. Having always been a football fan, she found herself even more enthralled getting to see the game this close. She could hear the hum of conversations on the sidelines though she couldn't hear the exact words, and the sound from the stands was so loud that it was almost deafening. She found herself cheering along whenever the Tornadoes gained yardage and sighing whenever they dropped balls or lost yards.

The game was going to be a close one. Both teams were evenly matched, and Clara found herself holding her breath every time Mason was thrown the ball. With just two minutes until halftime, she finally felt her body relax. There was only time for a few more plays and then he would be safe. At least during half time. And maybe she'd been wrong. He seemed to be okay; she couldn't see any noticeable limping.

Blaine stepped back, and she watched as he scanned the field for an open receiver. His right arm cocked back, and the ball went up in the air. She watched as it spun in a perfect spiral and sailed over the heads of the players in the middle of the field toward Mason who was close to the end zone. It was slightly over his head, and he had to jump to reach it. His hands closed around the ball and he tucked in like normal, but as he was coming down, a player from the opposing team ran into him.

Clara held her breath as he hit the ground. She couldn't tell if he had landed on his foot, but either way, it had looked to be a hard hit. The opposing player got up, but Mason stayed on the ground.

"No!" The word came out louder than she expected and Davis turned to look at her. She clapped her hand over her mouth to keep from shouting anything more and kept her eyes on the scene.

When it became obvious that Mason wasn't getting up, Justin headed out onto the field with the team doctor.

Clara wanted to rush out there as well, but as the newest trainer, that was not her place. Plus, it would announce her feelings for Mason to everyone in the stands, and after their interactions this week, she wasn't sure he'd be okay with that. So instead, she held her breath and watched.

The seconds seemed to drag on forever. Did it always take this long? Had he lost consciousness? She hadn't seen him hit his head but she supposed it was possible.

The players on the field circled around Mason and the doctors, blocking her view. Frustration coursed through her, and she clamped her teeth together to keep from yelling at them to move. Finally, the sea parted and a cheer rose up from the crowd. Mason was making his way over to the sidelines, but not by himself. His arms were slung over the shoulders of Justin and the doc, and only one foot was touching the ground as he made his way over. The other hung at an odd angle.

Before she could say anything to him, they disappeared into the medical tent that sat on the sidelines. Clara blew out another frustrated breath as she clenched and unclenched her fists at her side. Right now, she definitely hated those tents. She wanted to see what was happening, to know that he was okay.

The half ended and the tent stayed silent and impenetrable with no update on Mason. Reluctantly, she followed

Davis back into the locker room area. Hopefully, an update on Mason would come soon. She didn't think she'd be able to sit through the rest of the game if she didn't know what had happened to him.

"I sure hope he's okay," Davis said as they re-stocked the supplies on the tables. The area where they were was eerily quiet as the rest of the players were meeting with the coaches first before seeing them again.

"Me too." Clara hoped her voice didn't give her feelings away, but at this point, she cared less about that and more about finding out if he was okay.

The door opened, and she looked up, expecting to see the players coming in although it would signal a short meeting, but Justin's face appeared instead. It was tight and pinched in a way she hadn't ever seen it. That couldn't mean good news. "Clara, can I see you for a moment?"

Clara looked over at Davis with wide eyes before making her way to Justin. Was she in trouble? She didn't think she had done anything - she'd even told him her concerns - but she couldn't imagine why he would want to talk to her unless she was.

When they were safely outside the room and away from other ears, Justin swallowed and looked down at his hands. He cleared his throat as if the words were hard for him to utter. "Mason needs to go to the hospital, and he needs someone from the team to go with him. I have to stay here and finish the game, and since you're the newest hire and you suspected his injury beforehand, well that straw belongs to you."

Clara wasn't sure if he was chiding her or congratulating her for being right. She hadn't wanted to be right; she'd just wanted Mason to be safe. Whatever the connotation behind the words though, they were music to her ears. Now, she would finally know that he was okay, and she'd get to spend some time with him away from prying eyes.

Careful to keep her face from showing her emotion, she nodded. "Yes, sir, I understand. Is there anything else I should know?"

"Don't talk to the press and keep the cameras away from him. I think you were right and that he tore his Achilles, but if it isn't that bad, we don't want word of the injury getting out and them removing him from playing next game. If there is a next game."

He spoke as he walked, leading her toward the exit. By the time he reached the end of his sentence, they were at what appeared to be a back-door entrance of the stadium. Justin pushed open the door, and Clara saw the ambulance, silent and idling.

"He's inside. Go ahead and climb in back and remember, no press."

"Got it, but I didn't grab my bag. Can you make sure it gets taken care of?"

Justin nodded though his attention seemed to be elsewhere. "Sure, I'll have Davis take care of it."

Clara hoped he would, but she didn't feel like pushing the issue. Mason was what mattered right now. She knocked on the back door of the ambulance, and it swung open. An EMT offered her a hand up, and she sat down in a makeshift chair near Mason's head.

"Are you it, then?" the EMT asked.

"Yes, we can go now." Clara kept her eyes on Mason whose eyes were closed. Was he resting? Unconscious?

The back door shut, and the ambulance rolled forward. The movement stirred Mason, and his eyes flicked open. "Clara?"

She smiled and nodded. "It's me, Mace. I'm riding to the hospital with you."

"Good. I'm glad it's you. I love you, Clara." His words were soft and fuzzy as if he was speaking through a dream or a haze of pain.

She blinked, waiting for him to say more, but his eyes merely closed again. I love you too, Mason, she thought, but she couldn't bring herself to say the words out loud. Not yet.

Mason opened his eyes and blinked against the bright lights. Where was he? This was not his room. It was too white and too sterile. His own room was painted a soft blue and the walls were covered with framed pictures of famous players. These walls were pale and impersonal, and then he remembered. The injury. He tried to replay the scene in his mind, but all he could remember was jumping up for the catch and then landing all wrong.

He rolled his head to the side. Surely someone had come with him to the hospital. Maybe they would know more. A form was curled up in a chair, but it took him a moment to realize who it was. Clara? They had sent Clara to the hospital with him?

For a moment he wondered why, but he decided he didn't

care. He was actually glad it was Clara. Not only did he trust her, but he knew she would tell it to him straight. Besides, she looked beautiful there in the chair with her strawberry blonde hair spilling over her face.

As if sensing his gaze on her, she opened her eyes and blinked at him. "Oh, you're awake." She rubbed her eyes and yawned before stretching to a standing position.

"How long have I been out?" He had no concept of time. The room had no windows, and the bright lights made it feel like noon when he knew it had to be much later.

"A few hours. You were dazed when they brought you in, and then I think they gave you something for the pain." She touched the side of his bed as if wanting to touch his arm but afraid of what he might say or do. "Do you feel any pain?"

He closed his eyes and tried to assess his pain, but everything still felt a little hazy. "I'm not feeling much of anything right now." His eyes flicked to hers. "How bad is it though?"

When her teeth bit down on her bottom lip, and her eyes slid to the side, he knew it was bad.

"Am I out for the rest of the season?" This couldn't be happening. They had a chance at the Championship game again, and he wouldn't be able to play?

"I think so." Sadness creased her features even as concern filled her eyes.

"Did I at least hold on to the ball?"

She chuckled and shook her head. "Yeah, you did. I don't know if the team managed to score off it because I was a little busy being concerned about you, but you held onto the ball."

"You were concerned about me?" He didn't know why, but the words sent a thrill through his chest. If she was concerned, did that mean she still cared about him?

Her head tilted to the side, and tiny wrinkles furrowed her brow. Had he said something confusing?

"Of course, I was concerned about you. It's kind of my job."

Right. Her job. That was probably the only reason she was here as well. They'd probably made her come being lowest on the seniority pole.

"You don't remember anything after the catch?"

Why was she looking at him like that? Had he made a giant fool of himself somehow? "Not really. I vaguely remember hitting the ground, pain, and then waking up here."

"Oh." Was she disappointed? She sounded disappointed, but he had no idea why she would be.

"Did I do something? Say something that I should know about?"

She opened her mouth to speak and then sighed. "No, I'm sure it's nothing."

He was absolutely sure it was something, but as she didn't seem to want to talk about it, he decided not to push. It would probably come back to him sooner or later, and he could deal with the embarrassment then.

"So, how bad is it?" he asked, changing the topic. Her

face had already told him it was bad, but he needed to hear just how bad.

"The doctor hasn't been in yet, but I'm fairly certain it's torn, Mason. Your Achilles."

Torn. That was very bad news. He'd done enough research when he was looking up Achilles Tendonitis to know that his season was over and most of his summer would be spent in rehab. "Do you know my options?"

"It depends on how bad it is, but from what I understand there are two options. One is non-surgical but it might take a little longer and there are some increased chances of re-rupturing it. The other option is surgery. It's quicker but more painful and not without risk."

"Surgery it is then," Mason said as soon as she'd finished.

"But, Mason, there are risks with surgery too, and you'll still be out four to six months minimum."

Four to six months was not the news he wanted to hear. That would run right into summer training time. If he missed that, would they even play him next season? If he was lucky, he could catch the last few weeks or month of training camp, and maybe he'd get really lucky and heal faster. Or his recovery would go so smoothly that he'd be back at peak performance and they'd have to start him. "It's the best option to be able to play again. I'm already going to miss a lot of summer training camp. If I miss all of it, I may not get to play in the next season."

"Would that be so bad?" Her voice was so soft that he wasn't even sure he had heard her.

"I can't not play, Clara. It's all I've ever wanted."

She nodded, but he wasn't sure she understood. She had come from money. Her father had owned the biggest business in their hometown, and Clara had never wanted for anything. He, on the other hand, had grown up without much. He'd known hunger and frustration and how hard his parents had worked. He needed the money now, not only to feel secure, but to help his parents out. They had sacrificed so much for him.

The door opened, and a man in scrubs and a white coat appeared. "Ah, you're awake. That's good. How's the pain?" He sanitized his hands and then sat at the stool nearest the computer in the room.

Mason put on his best poker face. "Not bad right now, but I'm assuming it will get worse when the pain medication wears off."

The doctor nodded. "It will be sore for sure, but depending on the route we take, we'll get you some medication to help with any pain."

Mason struggled to sit up and make himself seem assertive. It was rather hard to do in a hospital gown, especially when his legs still felt a little like Jell-O. "I want surgery. As soon as possible."

The doctor blinked at him, and then looked over at Clara

who shrugged. "We haven't even performed the MRI yet. We have to do that before I can discuss options."

His hand clenched the thin sheet covering him. "I'm a professional athlete, doc. I need to be able to play. Is surgery my best option?"

The doctor turned on the stool and stared evenly at Mason before nodding. "Depending on the tear and what the MRI shows, then yes, possibly."

Mason lifted his chin and stared evenly at the doctor. "Then let's get the MRI and see what it shows."

"I'll get it scheduled." He tapped for a few minutes on the keyboard, pushed back from the stool, and then left the room.

Mason tried to settle back and relax, but it was impossible. His mind kept racing through the scenarios and 'what if' questions. He knew he would have to be patient, but that was easier said than done.

❧ 15 ☙

CLARA

C lara used the time Mason was removed from the room for his MRI to check in with Justin. She had no idea if the game was finished yet or if he would even answer, but she needed to get the information to someone.

The phone rang in her ear, and voicemail picked up. "Justin, it's Clara. Mason just went in for an MRI, but it is torn. They're going to try to rush him into surgery tonight depending on the MRI, but I know the team was planning on heading back. Will they wait for us or do we need to find another way home? Could you call me when you get this?"

She hung up the phone and sank down into the guest chair in Mason's room. This was a nightmare. They were at an unfamiliar hospital with no transportation and hundreds of miles from home. How would they even get home if the team left without them? Would the team leave without them? She didn't think so, but then she'd never been in this situation before. She wished she had her Bible for comfort.

Her Bible! While she didn't have the book, she did have an app on her phone. At least she could read a little while she waited and try to take all these worries to God. She knew He said to cast all cares upon Him, but in a situation like this, that was easier said than done. With the app pulled up, she searched for verses on comfort and began to read them earnestly. She was still immersed in them when the door opened and Mason was wheeled back in.

"Well, I've got good news," the doctor said as he entered behind Mason. "It's only a partial tear, and I don't think surgery is necessary. We'll get him put in an ankle cast to stabilize the ankle, and he should see a therapy specialist in the next two days to get a special heeled boot."

"That is good news," Clara said, standing and pocketing her phone. "What does the recovery time look like with this option?"

"The specialist will be able to tell you more, but I would say four to eight weeks."

Four to eight weeks. That still ended his season, but it would allow him to do camp in the summer. Though Clara knew Mason wouldn't be thrilled to have to sit out the rest of the playoff games, this was better than she'd expected.

"Thank you, sir. Will he be able to get the cast soon?"

"I'll have someone come in right away. Should take about

half an hour to apply it and then once it hardens enough, we can release him."

"Thank you." As the doctor left the room, Clara approached Mason's bed. "Did you hear that? Four to eight weeks?"

"Yeah, it still means I'm out for the rest of the season though."

"It does, but it means summer is possible. This is the best news we could have hoped for." She grabbed his hand and squeezed.

Mason shook his head. "I should have listened to you, Clara. I'm sorry."

Clara flashed a small smile. "It's okay. I understand why you didn't, and I promise I will be there with you every step of the way to help you recover."

Mason nodded, but before he could say anything else, a nurse entered. She was a short woman with reddish brown hair and a kind smile. In front of her, she pushed a small cart laden with different materials that Clara could only assume would come together to form a cast. Clara stepped back to allow her to work.

"Got a little tear I heard? Did you at least win the game?" The nurse's voice faltered between curiosity and teasing as she pulled up a stool and adjusted the cart with her supplies.

Mason looked to Clara, but she shook her head. She'd been way too worried about Mason to pay attention to the game. "Uh, I don't know yet. I'll see if I can find out."

Clara pulled out her phone and tapped the icon for the internet. The signal bar flashed, indicating she was not getting good reception. Hospitals were the worst. Stepping closer to the door, she held the phone up as if she could beam a better signal that way. Finally, the page loaded and she quickly tapped information to find the score. "Aha, we won. Twenty-four to twenty-one."

"That's decent," the nurse said with a nod as her hands fitted a gauze-like sleeve over Mason's ankle. "Must have been a pretty even matchup."

"Well, it is the playoffs," Mason said. "Too bad I won't be playing the next game."

The nurse smiled as if she understood his moody tone. "There will always be another game. My son plays basketball, and he broke his pinky of all things and not even playing ball. Ruined the rest of his season, but I told him the same thing. There's always next season."

Clara could tell the words held no comfort for Mason, but he'd have to find a way to see the bright side. Otherwise, his next few weeks would be full of dark feelings and bitterness.

Fifteen minutes later, the nurse finished and pushed back. "I'll get you some crutches and your discharge paperwork. Once the doctor signs off, you can be on your way. It might be a good time to line up transportation."

Right. Transportation. Justin still hadn't returned her phone call. She decided to try texting him instead. "Mason's tear isn't bad. No surgery needed. Just got a cast and waiting for crutches. Can someone pick us up?"

Her phone vibrated a minute later with his response. "Good news. Sending van. Team waiting."

Well, at least the man was better at returning texts than he was at returning phone calls. "The team is sending a van for us."

Mason grunted in response and shrugged his shoulders.

Clara stepped forward and placed a hand on his shoulder. "Mason, I know this isn't what you wanted, but you'll still be at every game. Try to find the bright side in this. It will make it much easier to get through."

He sighed and looked up at her. "You're right. This just wasn't how I imagined my week going. First, you and I get in a fight, then this injury." He shook his head. "I just thought it would be different this time."

"Okay, here you go," the nurse said, re-entering the room and interrupting the moment. "I have crutches for you. No weight on that foot until they get you fitted with a heeled boot." She handed the wieldy instruments to Mason and then turned to Clara. "Here are the discharge and care papers. The doctor wants an appointment with a specialist no later than Tuesday."

"Understood," Clara said as she took the papers.

"And, I've even called you a chariot to deliver you to the front door." She pointed to the man who had entered behind her and the wheelchair in front of him.

Mason clenched his jaw as he stood and hobbled over to the wheelchair. Clara knew it was taking every ounce of his strength not to insist he could walk out of the hospital. She also knew it was policy. Every patient was wheeled out.

"Remember what I said," the nurse said, patting Mason's shoulder before heading for the door. She paused at the entrance and turned. "I hope you win the Championship again."

"Thank you," Clara called after her as Mason remained mute. "You could have at least thanked her," she said to him as the orderly pushed him out of the room.

Mason said nothing as they made their way to the entrance of the hospital. The sliding glass doors slid open and the orderly wheeled Mason to the curb. Clara was afraid they'd be waiting in tense silence, but just then a white van pulled up to the curb.

"That must be our ride," Clara said as the driver stepped out and opened the side door. She watched as the driver and the orderly helped load Mason into the back seat. Her eyes followed their movements, hoping she would be able to reproduce them when they reached the airport and he had to be unloaded. After a few moments, they had him situated with his back leaned against the window, so his foot could be propped up on the seat.

Satisfied that he was okay, she climbed into the front seat and buckled her seat belt. As she clutched the papers the nurse had given her, she hoped that Justin or Davis had gathered up *her* bag when they'd loaded up the supplies. She'd reminded Justin to, but she had a feeling his mind had been elsewhere at the time. Still, Davis appeared much calmer, and she was sure he had noticed her things and taken care of them.

Mason made no move to converse on the ride, and though the mood in the van was tense, the ride itself was peaceful. Clara almost engaged the driver, but she was enjoying the silence too much. She knew there would be little of that when she got on the plane. Everyone would want to know all about his injury, and she was sure she would have to have a meeting with Justin to figure out a plan of action for him going forward.

Justin, Blaine, the team doctor, and the head coach were all waiting outside the plane when the van pulled up. Clara opened the door as soon as it stopped and jogged over to meet them. "He's going to need help getting out of the van and into the plane. They don't want him putting any weight on the foot for seventy-two hours."

"And after that?" the coach asked.

"We need to set an appointment with a specialist to fit him for a boot, but the doctor was hopeful that with rehab he would recover in four to eight weeks."

"Four to eight weeks?"

She was surprised at his shock. Surely, Mason was not the first athlete he'd coached to have torn an Achilles, and honestly had his tear been any worse, he would be having surgery and be out for months instead of weeks. Perhaps it had been long enough since the coach had seen a similar injury that he simply thought medical and rehab efforts had improved.

"We'll have to play Jefferson more and get Toby up to speed," Blaine said.

"We'll figure all that out when we get back," the coach agreed with a nod of his head. "Let's get Mason loaded up, so we can get home."

The plane ride back was less eventful than Clara had thought it would be. Most of the men appeared too tired to grill Mason much. After a few questions that he answered with short clipped responses, Mason and many of the other players passed out. Clara curled up in her own chair and let the weariness of the day take over.

It felt like she had barely closed her eyes when she heard the familiar ding and the lights came on in the cabin. She rubbed her eyes to adjust to the new brightness. After blinking a few times to clear the fuzziness, she turned her wrist toward her to check the time. It was after midnight. She sure hoped Justin would allow a late start to today's work because she wasn't sure she'd make it to an eight am meeting.

"I know it's a lot to ask, but can you take Mason to his house?" Justin asked from the seat across from hers. He too was stretching and attempting to get his bearings. "I would do it myself, but I'm going to need to be at an early meeting to discuss his rehab."

Clara stood and rolled her shoulders back to loosen the kinks. "I had already planned on it. I'll make sure he gets set up and I'll arrange for his car to be returned to his place tomorrow."

"Good." Justin nodded, absently. "Since the two of you seemed to work well together, do you want to take the lead on his rehab?"

A flutter of excitement stirred in her chest at the thought of spending more one on one time with Mason, but she tried to keep her face from showing it. "I'd be happy to."

"Great. You'll be checking in with me, of course, but I know the team is going to want him back as soon as possible, and that's only going to work if he has consistent training happening."

"Understand. I meant to ask earlier, but did you or Davis grab my bag from the stadium?"

"Yeah, we grabbed everything. I'm sure it's with our bags."

Clara nodded, yawned once more, and headed toward the front of the plane with the rest of the players. After several more minutes of standing around and scanning the bags to make sure they had everything, the team loaded up into the waiting shuttle.

An hour later, the shuttle dropped them off at the Tornado

facility, and forty-five minutes after that, she was pulling into the driveway of Mason's house.

Though exhaustion covered her like a blanket, she forced her eyes to stay open and appear alert. He had to be even more tired than she was, and she would do him no good if she fell asleep before getting him settled.

After parking the car, she grabbed the crutches and then helped Mason out. He still hadn't spoken much, but a grimace of pain was etched in his face now. She wished the doctor had given her some pills for the pain, and she made a mental note to ask for some at his next appointment.

"Just a little bit farther. We'll get you set up in bed and then you can get some rest."

His response was a grunt, but he crutched his way up the sidewalk to his front door. When they reached it, he began trying to fumble in his pockets while remaining upright, and Clara had visions of him falling over or stepping down on his foot.

"Let me," she said, placing a hand on his arm to still him.

He held her gaze a moment before returning his hand to the crutch handle and letting her reach down into his pocket.

Clara's face heated up as she stepped closer and fished out the keys. She was so close to him that she could almost hear his heart beating in time with hers. His breath tickled her cheek, and the scent of him, masked as it was by the lingering smell of hospital and antiseptic, burned in her nose.

"Which one?" she asked as the ring of keys escaped his

pocket and jingled in her hand. Her eyes flicked up to his, and her breath caught in her throat at the way he was looking at her.

"The gold one." His voice was soft and scratchy, and she wondered if he was fighting the same emotions she was. She dared not continue to look at him in case he was.

With trembling fingers, she inserted the key, turned the lock, and pushed the door open. His house inside was dark and quiet, and she fumbled around for a switch. Finding it, she flipped it on, and light burst through the room.

Though she'd been there once before, she took a moment to glance around the room again. It was a modest living room with a large fireplace and an even larger TV. A leather couch faced the sleek screen as did a recliner. Pictures of famous players from a variety of teams adorned the walls. It was a man's living room to be sure, and she felt a small smile tug at her lips at the complete lack of a woman's touch which led her to believe he wasn't seeing anyone.

"I don't think you should try to make it to the bedroom tonight. How's the couch? Is it comfortable? I can get you sheets and whatever you need." She clamped her mouth shut to keep the rambling words from spilling out.

Mason flashed her a half smile. "Yeah, it's comfortable. I've got shorts in my bag that I'm fine to sleep in, but some sheets would be nice. They're in the closet at the top of the stairs."

Clara nodded and headed that direction. She was curious

as to what the rest of his house looked like, but now was not the time to go exploring. There would be plenty of time for that later as she was fairly certain she'd be spending a lot of time here with him.

The linen closet at the top of the stairs was large but sparse. A few towels filled one shelf and two sets of sheets and blankets filled another. The other shelves were empty. She wondered if that was because he hadn't lived here long or because he just didn't have the need to fill them. Pushing the thought aside for now, she grabbed a set of sheets and a blanket. She saw no pillow in the closet, and she didn't want to intrude on his bedroom without permission, so she returned without one, hoping he had some on the couch.

He was sitting in the recliner with both legs propped up when she re-entered the room, and she quickly made up the couch with the sheets. There were indeed two pillows on the couch and she placed them at one end for his head before adding the blanket and folding it down for him.

"Okay, I think you're good for tonight. Do you need anything else?" She tried not to look directly in his eyes for fear of what she might see there, but the pull was magnetic. An intensity flowed out of his gaze, but she wasn't quite sure what the emotion was.

"I think I'm good for now. Thank you for all your help, Clara."

"Of course." She bit her lip as she thought of what else to say. The silence screamed for something. "Well, I should let you go, but I've been assigned to head up your rehab, so I'll check in with you later today. Call me if you need anything."

He nodded and though she felt like she should say more, that they should discuss this tension happening between them, now was not the time. There would be plenty of time for discussion later, so after flashing a small wave, she turned and walked out of his house.

When the door closed behind her, she took a moment to lean against it and take a deep breath. This was going to be a lot harder than she'd thought. Especially if he kept looking at her with that intense gaze that made her think he wanted to kiss her.

16

MASON

Mason woke stiff and sore the next morning. It took him a second to remember why, but once he opened his eyes and realized he was on his couch and not in his bed, it came crashing back. The pain registered then, along with a gnawing hunger in his belly. Though much of the day before remained a blur, he was fairly certain he hadn't eaten since before the game.

Reaching for the crutches, he took a steadying breath and then pulled himself up to a standing position. The room swam, and he closed his eyes tightly until it subsided. When it stilled, he began the slow, hobbling walk to the kitchen. He was certainly glad he was a minimalist and nothing lay on the floor for him to maneuver around because the crutches were awkward enough as it was. He wasn't used to having to depend on anything other than his own two feet.

Coffee was the first thing on his agenda, but he hadn't realized how much harder it would be to make with basically only one free hand. He was forced to lean one crutch against the bar and practically hop around with the other in order to take the grounds to the coffee pot. He was doubly thankful that his coffee pot was next to his sink when he realized hopping around with a glass pot filled with water would be dangerous and disastrous. How was he going to do simple things by himself if making coffee was so hard?

"Knock, knock."

The sound of Clara's voice jolted him so much that he almost spilled the water anyway. How did she get in? He was certain he hadn't given her a key.

"Hope I didn't startle you," she said as she appeared in the kitchen. "The front door was still unlocked."

Ah, yes, he'd never locked the door after she left. To be fair, he had been exhausted and in too much pain, but it was a good thing he lived in a safe neighborhood.

"Do you need help?" Her face folded in concern as she took in his precarious stance and only one crutch. Within seconds, she was by his side, handing him the other crutch and taking the coffee pot from him. "Why don't you go sit down and I'll take care of this?"

He wanted to object, to tell her that he could do it himself, but the truth was that he couldn't. Well, perhaps he could, but it would have taken twice as long and his ankle was already throbbing. "Thank you."

"Of course. I didn't even think about how hard it might be to get around in the kitchen with two crutches. I'll look today to see if they have one of those scooters you can place your knee on. At least then you'll have the use of both arms for things like this." She poured the water into the machine and pressed the button. After a few grunting and grinding noises, the soft sounds of coffee dripping into the pot filled the air.

"Have you eaten?" she asked, barely missing a beat.

"No." He eased himself down into a chair at the table and sighed. "I was going to have cereal after I got the coffee started, but I realize that would be hard to do as well."

"Cereal?" Her nose wrinkled as if he'd just said something offensive. "You can't just have cereal. How about I make you an omelet or some eggs and bacon instead?" Before he had a chance to say anything, she was opening the fridge and rummaging around.

He chuckled at her take charge attitude. She might have changed a little since they had dated, but this personality trait definitely hadn't faded. If anything, it might even be more pronounced, but somehow, he didn't mind her taking care of him. He hated not being able to take care of himself, but having Clara around definitely wasn't the worst thing in the world.

"Okay, if you want. I certainly won't turn down a hot breakfast."

"Good." Without missing a beat, she found a pan and

started the bacon. Though she had only been here once before, she looked completely at ease in his kitchen. As the bacon sizzled, she rummaged in the cabinets for mugs, pulling two down and filling one with coffee for him and the other for herself. She added milk to her coffee, and then, without asking, she emptied two packets of sugar in his coffee - just the way he liked it - before setting it down in front of him.

He stared up at her. "You remembered." She hadn't made coffee for him in years, but she hadn't forgotten the way he liked it.

Her face flushed, and she shrugged. "It's an easy order to remember."

While that was true, the color on her face suggested there was more than that behind it. He bit back his smile and sipped the warm liquid. Could they try dating again? He still wasn't sure exactly why they had split up in the first place, but he was starting to wonder if it mattered anymore. She'd claimed she didn't want to hold him back, but that had made no sense to him at the time. She could never do that, and while there had to be a reason, he was no longer sure the reason was as important as he'd always made it out to be.

He watched her bustle around his kitchen and realized he wanted to try again. He'd been lonelier than he'd known and having someone take care of him pointed a spotlight on that feeling.

"You mind if I join you?" she asked as she placed two

plates on the table and handed him a fork. "I wanted to check on you first thing so I kind of skipped breakfast."

"Aw, were you worried about me?"

"A little," Clara said with a shrug. "You were pretty quiet yesterday."

"Yeah, it was a rough day. I thought about what you said though about looking for the bright side, and I want you to know that I'm trying."

Her eyes shifted from his and down to her plate. "How about we pray and eat this before it gets cold?"

After praying, they ate in silence, each lost in their own worlds. When they were both finished, she cleared the plates and placed them in the sink. "I have to run into work for a bit, but I don't want you to worry about these dishes. I'll wash them when I come back. Until then, I want you to relax back on the couch. Watch some television or something. Your rehab will start in a few days, and you'll be busy enough then. You might as well take the day to rest."

He smiled at her mothering tone but didn't fight her. "Okay, but let me give you something first."

A look of curiosity alighted on her face, but she followed him back to the living room. He picked up his key ring from where she had placed it last night and pulled the house key off. Then he held it out to her. "I get the feeling you'll not only be here a lot but will need to come and go often."

Shaking her head, she held up her hand and took a step back. "I can't take that, Mason. I can just ring the bell."

He tilted his head forward and fixed her with a pointed look. "And wait for me to hobble over to open it? What happens if I'm asleep or heaven forbid, I fall and injure myself again? I would feel better knowing you could get in if you needed to."

Hesitation tightened her features, and she chewed on her bottom lip but finally agreed. "Okay, I'll take it, but only because it makes you feel better. Now, please rest. I'll be back as soon as I can with the scooter, and maybe if you're good, I'll order pizza tonight."

His lips curved in a smile at the mention of their old joke. Always an athlete, his diet rarely afforded him the luxury of pizza, at least during the season. Only on rare occasions when he'd felt it was extra special had he indulged. With his playing time ended for the foreseeable future, now seemed like the perfect time for the hot cheesy goodness. "Well, I certainly won't say no to that. I'll be on my best behavior." He crossed his fingers over his chest and then held them up like he was being sworn in.

She helped him get re-situated on the couch and brought him a large bottle of water before promising again to return as soon as she could.

When the front door closed behind her, Mason flicked on the TV, but he couldn't keep his thoughts from returning to the beautiful strawberry blonde and the promise of her return.

From his bag came the buzzing sound of his phone. He reached down and fished the phone out, unsurprised to see his parent's number on the screen. They had probably been calling him since the accident yesterday. In fact, he was surprised they hadn't sent Duke over to gather information for them.

"Hey Mom, Dad," he said, putting the phone to his ear.

"Mason David Dixon, how dare you not call us to let us know you were okay?" His mother's voice was shrill and filled with more anger than he'd ever heard in it before.

Mason sighed. "Mom, I was rushed to the hospital from the stadium. I didn't have my phone. By the time I got home, it was nearly two in the morning."

"I don't care what time it is; you call your mother when you get injured on national TV. I was up half the night worried about you. I must have called you every hour on the hour, and Duke didn't seem to know what was going on either. Does that team not alert your family?"

"I'm sure they would have had it been more serious," Mason began but his mother cut him off before he could finish.

"And how serious is it?"

"It's a partial tear in my Achilles tendon, Mom." Mason rubbed his hand across his forehead. He loved his mother, but sometimes she was so overbearing. "They put on an ankle cast, and the doctor said it will take four to eight weeks to recover."

"Four to eight weeks? I'm coming to help."

Mason's head shot up. The thought of his mother

crowding in his space for two months was not only terrifying, but it was not happening. "No, Mom, I'm fine. I've got Duke close by, and Clara is checking in on me."

"Clara? Your ex-girlfriend, Clara?" The tone in her voice had shifted, but he wasn't exactly sure what the new tone was. Disbelief? Condescension?

"She's an athletic trainer for the team, Mom. She was with me at the hospital yesterday, and she'll be checking in on me until I'm cleared to play again."

"Can't you get someone else?" his mother asked, and he thought he could finally place the tone. Distrust? He supposed that was natural since Clara had broken his heart.

"No, I can't get someone else, Mother. That's not how it works in pro football. She's the trainer assigned to me, and I can't just tell them I don't want to work with her." Besides, he *did* want to work with her. If he had just listened to her, he might not be in this situation.

"Promise me you'll be careful then, Mason. You know what happened last time with her."

Except that was the problem. He didn't know what happened last time. Not really, but he was determined to find out.

17

CLARA

It was early afternoon when Clara arrived at the training facility. Justin had told her she could come in late, but she hoped he had actually meant it. Her body had needed the rest for sure, and she was glad she had made the stop to check on Mason as well. Otherwise, his morning might have been disastrous.

"Ah, there you are," Justin said as soon as she entered the training office. "I was hoping you would make it in today to give me an update."

"Sorry, I'm late. It was a rather late night. I got Mason situated last night or rather early this morning." It had been nearly two am when she'd finally gotten back to her own place. "I stopped by on my way here as well, and I think we need to get him one of those scooters. He was trying to make coffee and hop around with one crutch." She shook her head. "It was comical, but it was also dangerous."

Justin ran a hand across his chin. "I see. Well, we can certainly get him one of those. How about his pain?"

"He was definitely feeling more today than yesterday, but it didn't seem unbearable. We do need to get him an appointment to get fitted for a boot though."

"If I give you the doctor's number, can you take care of that? I know caring for him wasn't really what you signed up for, but it sounds like he's going to need some full time help for a while."

Clara nodded. "Of course, sir, whatever I can do to help."

"Great, let's see if we can find one of those scooters, and then I'll get you the doctor's number."

She followed him to the athletic training closet where they kept most of their supplies. After a bit of rummaging around, they managed to find a scooter. It was older and dusty from no use, but it was functional and would keep him from falling over while he tried to make food.

"You might ask for a better one when you take him in for his appointment, but this will do until then."

"Thank you, sir. I'll get that appointment set now."

When her stomach began rumbling a few hours later, she performed a final check to make sure she hadn't missed anybody she needed to see - Justin had lightened her load to allow her more time to check on Mason, but she didn't want to miss anything. Then she grabbed the scooter and headed out to her favorite pizza place to grab a pie to go.

Half an hour later, she was pulling into Mason's driveway, the garlic and sauce smell from the pizza sending her stomach rumbling into overdrive. Her mouth watered as she tucked the scooter under one arm and held the pizza box carefully in the other.

At the front door, she had to put the scooter down to engage the key. Using it still felt awkward, especially since they weren't a couple, but it was certainly easier than trying to ring the bell and waiting for him to appear.

When the lock turned, she pushed the door open and set the pizza box down on a nearby table in order to retrieve the scooter. "Mason, it's Clara," she hollered as she entered. Perhaps announcing herself would feel a little less awkward.

"Come on in." His muffled voice carried in from another room.

She set the scooter down, locked the door behind her, and picked up the pizza box again before continuing into the kitchen. A moment later, Mason appeared from a hallway she assumed led to a bathroom.

"That smells delicious, and I am famished."

"Good, why don't you take a seat, and I'll get us some plates and drinks."

With a soft smile, Mason held up his hands in surrender and sat down at the table. "You know I feel bad just sitting here and making you do all the work."

Clara tossed him a teasing smile before pulling two plates out of the cupboard. "Well, I brought a scooter home for you, so tomorrow all bets are off."

"Is that right?"

Clara took the plates to the table and then grabbed two Cokes from the fridge. "The scooter is not a free pass, just so you know. It's to help you get around; it is not an excuse to be stupid."

A look of mock shock covered Mason's face. "I would never."

She set the Cokes down, folded her arms, and fixed him with a pointed stare. Did he really think she didn't remember all the stupid things he had done in high school? "Oh, yes, you would. I remember that time in high school when you decided to jump between the roofs of the sheds at my house just to see if you could. You almost fell and broke a leg then."

Mason's smile widened as he chuckled. "Okay, that was pretty stupid. As was the time I tried truck bed surfing with Derek."

Clara's eyes widened. "You did what? Never mind, I don't want to know. I'm sure the visual in my head right now is close enough."

A deep laugh barreled out of Mason's throat. "Probably. Is that why you really broke up with me? You were afraid I'd do something stupid and sully your name?"

Though he was teasing, his words hit like a punch to

Clara's face, and her smile faltered. "Mason, no, of course not."

His own smile fell as he realized the mood had changed. "Then, why, Clara? I've always wondered. You said it was because you would hold me back, but we both know that's not the truth."

Clara sighed. She didn't want to get into the conversation with him now. In fact, she wasn't sure she ever wanted to, but this was the second time he'd asked, and she couldn't keep putting him off forever. "Mason, it was so long ago."

"But you have to still remember. I mean you're the one who broke it off. There had to have been a reason. Maybe it's stupid, but I need to know."

There was a reason. There definitely was. But telling Mason that her father hadn't wanted them together, and that he'd offered to pay for Mason's college if she broke it off wasn't going to make him feel any better. She hated lying, but maybe a small lie would end the discussion for now.

She took a deep breath. "I'd always heard that relationships grew strained during college years. Especially if the two people went to different colleges. I know it was kind of selfish, but I wanted to enjoy that time, and I wanted you to as well."

Mason's eyes bored into hers as if searching for her truthfulness. While that wasn't the whole truth, it was what she had told herself when she broke things off. She'd continued telling herself those words so often that they felt a lot like the truth.

"I guess that sort of makes sense, though I have to tell you, I would have enjoyed college more with you by my side."

She felt the same way, but she wasn't sure telling him that right now would be the right thing to do. Instead, she decided to change the subject. "Your pizza's getting cold."

Mason narrowed his eyes at her, and she could tell they would be discussing this more later, but he agreed to drop the topic. For now. "Fine. Do you want to pray for us?"

Clara bowed her head. "Lord, thank you for this food and for good company. Please help Mason's injury heal quickly, so he can get back to what he loves. Amen."

"Amen," Mason echoed.

They ate their pizza in silence, but Clara couldn't help sneaking glances in his direction. She had thought she was doing the best thing for him when she'd agreed to break up with him, but now she wasn't so sure. What if they could have made it work? What if he could have gone to college without her father's money?

"What are you thinking?" Mason asked, catching her staring at him.

"I was thinking that we should watch a movie. What do you have around here?" Clara busied herself with removing their plates and putting away the leftover pizza.

"It's the twenty-first century, Clara. I can pretty much get anything on demand."

Right. She knew that. Though she was living more modestly now, she'd grown up with money and her father had bought every channel he could. Now, he had probably added all the apps as well. Heaven forbid he miss his favorite show.

"Okay then, what have you been wanting to see?" She cleared the last of the remaining trash from the table and handed him his crutches.

He narrowed his eyes at her. "Really? You'll watch anything I want to watch?"

"Sure, why wouldn't I?"

"Because you never let me choose the movie in high school," he said with a laugh. "You always made me watch those sappy Hallmark love stories which I did because I cared for you, but if it's my choice…" he shrugged, "then we're watching Rocky."

"Rocky? Are you kidding me? That movie is old."

"It's not old. It's a classic."

She pushed his shoulder lightly. "Classic is just another word for old."

"Hey now, you better watch it." He halted his movement and turned to face her, but his voice still held it's teasing tone.

Clara couldn't help the wide grin that split her lips. "Oh yeah? Why? I'm pretty sure I can run faster than you right now." She darted to her left and then to her right, but she had misjudged how long Mason's arms were, and he caught her arm as she passed him.

She had no idea how he managed to do it on crutches, but somehow, he not only kept his balance, but managed to pull her close to his chest. His eyes stared down into hers. "Cheater. It's not fair to kick a man while he's down."

Her breath caught in her throat, as her gaze collided with his. "You don't seem to be a man down at the moment."

"Well, they do pay me for my skills with my hands as well as my feet." His eyes were burning through her with an intensity she hadn't felt in years.

"Do you have any other skills they pay you for?" She couldn't believe the words had left her mouth. Was she flirting with him? What did that mean? What did she hope to gain from it?

The corner of his mouth twitched. "Not that they pay me for, but I happen to think I'm skilled at one more thing."

She shouldn't ask. She could tell from the look in his eyes exactly what he was referring to, but she couldn't seem to stop her mouth from forming the words. "And what is that?"

He lowered his head, and his lips touched hers. Tingles raced across her lips, out across her cheeks, and down her spine. She'd kissed a few men since she and Mason had broken up, but none of them made her feel like this. Before she could rein in her racing heart and respond, he had pulled back.

"So, are you ready for that movie?" His eyes danced with laughter as he stared at her.

He was teasing her, and she wanted to slap him for it, but she was also kind of glad he had pulled back. She needed to figure out what she wanted before she lost herself again. "Absolutely."

18

MASON

Mason could not help replaying that kiss in his mind. He had no idea why he had done it. Clara had broken his heart once already and he really didn't need to feel that pain again, but she'd been so darn cute standing there in front of him. She'd smiled that tilted smile and he hadn't been able to help himself. And it had been just as amazing as he'd known it would be. The question was where did that leave them now? Were they a couple again? Would she wake up tomorrow thinking it had been a mistake?

"Are you going to put the movie on or not?" Clara teased him as she took a seat on the far end of the couch.

"I'm working on it. Are you really going to sit that far away?"

She folded her arms across her chest. "I wanted to give

you space to prop up your foot. You are supposed to be taking it easy, remember?"

Mason chuckled as he turned on the TV and the movie app. "How could I forget? You barely let me do anything."

"Oh, speaking of which," she said, jumping up from the couch and hurrying to the front door. "I brought this back for you today." She motioned to the scooter like she was one of the show girls on The Price is Right and he had just won a new car. "It's a little old, but we'll get you a newer one when we go to your appointment tomorrow if they have one."

"What appointment?" Mason knew the night before had been fuzzy but he was pretty sure she had never mentioned an appointment before.

"The one with your doctor that I set up earlier this afternoon. You have to be fitted for a boot. I've heard they aren't sexy, but it will help you start walking sooner."

The thought of a walking boot looking sexy on anyone curled Mason's lips into a smile. "If it's going to help me walk sooner, I don't care if it's old and ugly. Hey, bring that over here. I can prop my foot on it, and you can sit a little closer to me."

Clara narrowed her eyes at him but complied. "Just as long as you don't try any funny business, mister. You're still my charge."

Mason made the motion of a cross over his heart with his finger. "I promise. No funny business here."

Clara rolled her eyes but sat down in the middle of the

couch this time instead of on the other end. Mason bit back a smile as the movie started. If this was anything like high school, she'd be curled up against his chest before the first half of the movie was over. Though Clara loved movies, she had the worst habit of falling asleep in the middle of them and begging him to re-watch it so she could see the end.

He remembered how much that used to bug him, but he didn't think it would so much now. Now, he would give anything just to have her closer to him, to feel her body heat and the soft tickle of her hair on his arm.

Her hand lay just inches from his, and while it wasn't as nice as having his arm around her, it would do for now. Hoping she wouldn't push him away, he reached out and laced his fingers through hers. She smiled up at him and scooted a little closer.

They watched half of the movie that way and though Mason had picked it, he really wasn't paying much attention to it. He was much more focused on the beautiful woman beside him and how he could convince her to give them another shot. Before he could make another move, her cell phone rang in her pocket.

She jumped, pulling her hand away from him as she reached into her pocket. "Sorry, I have to get this. I'm sure it's work." But as she spied the caller ID, her face shifted. Her finger paused over the button as if she didn't want to answer it, but after a deep breath she pressed down. "Hi, Dad. What can I do for you?"

Her father? No wonder she hadn't wanted to answer the phone. Her father had been overbearing in high school, always dictating what Clara could do, where she could and couldn't go. Mason had even wondered if her father had tried to break them up, but he'd never been able to prove it. From the sound of her voice, Clara's relationship with him was still rocky.

"Nothing, Dad. Just watching a movie."

Mason's brow lifted. Just watching a movie? Why hadn't she mentioned him? Was she embarrassed? Did she think her father wouldn't approve?

"Now's not really a good time, Dad. Work is keeping me busy. One of the players was injured, and I'm in charge of the rehab." She turned her head slightly and mouthed the word sorry at him.

He knew her sorry was about having the conversation in front of him, but he was much more concerned with the fact that she wouldn't say his name. She hadn't told her father she was with him or that he was the injured player she was working with, and he had to know why. If she couldn't even tell her father about him, how could they try to rekindle their relationship?

"Sure, Dad, see you soon." She ended the call and shoved the phone back in her pocket. "Sorry about that. I would have ignored the call, but sometimes he gets worse when I do that."

"Why did you lie to him?" Mason's voice held an icy note.

Her eyes widened, and she blinked at him in surprise. "What do you mean? I didn't lie to him."

"Just watching a movie?"

"We are just watching a movie," she said as if that was all there was to it.

"Yeah, but you didn't tell him you were here with me. You couldn't even tell him I'm the injured player you're working with. Does he even know you took a job with the team I play for?" The pitch of his voice rose as the words flew out of his mouth. He knew he was being a little irrational but he couldn't seem to stop it.

The aversion of her gaze as she bit her lip told him the answer was no. "It wasn't important that he knew." Her voice was so quiet, he doubted she was even convincing herself.

Mason crossed his arms. "You don't think it's important that the man who drove us apart years ago knows that you're working closely with me?"

Exasperated, Clara threw her hands up. "He's not the one who drove us apart."

Mason quirked a brow. "Really? You can't even tell him you're with me and you expect me to believe he didn't tear us apart? That he had nothing to do with you breaking up with me?"

"He didn't," Clara said, but Mason knew she was lying. He could see it in the tell she'd always had, the slight pursing of her lips before she spoke. He'd tried to teach her to play poker once, but even after telling her what her tell was, she hadn't been able to keep from doing it every time she tried to bluff.

Mason shook his head. How had he been so wrong? "I thought we were rekindling something here, Clara, but it will never work out if you can't even tell him you're here with me."

"It was just a kiss, Mason."

Just a kiss? The words were a slap in his face. "It wasn't just a kiss to me, Clara. I've always known our breakup was wrong, but I hadn't realized how much I've missed you until you came into my life again."

"Mason, I…" she paused as if struggling for the right words to say, "I don't know if a relationship is a good thing right now."

"Obviously it isn't," Mason retorted, "since that kiss was 'just a kiss' to you."

"Okay, that was a poor choice of words," Clara began.

"No, I think it's exactly what you meant," Mason said, interrupting her. "I obviously didn't mean as much to you back then as you did to me, and I certainly don't now."

"Mason, that's not-"

"It's fine, really. I'm kind of tired, so maybe we should call this an early night." He wasn't tired in the least, but he was emotionally drained and he didn't feel like continuing the conversation any longer.

"Are you sure?" Clara looked as if she wanted to argue but wasn't sure what to say.

"Yeah, I'm sure."

She held his gaze a moment longer, and he saw the silent question in her eyes. The one that asked him if they were going to be okay, but he didn't have an answer for her because he didn't know.

She let out a frustrated sigh and nodded. "Okay, I'll be back at ten in the morning to take you to your appointment."

"Sure, sounds good." It sounded about as fun as a root canal at the moment, but perhaps he could convince Justin to send someone else instead. Although, then he might have to explain why he didn't want Clara, and he didn't feel like doing that either. What a mess!

With a final longing look, she grabbed her purse and exited the front door.

19

MASON

"Do you want to tell me why I'm taking you to this appointment and not one of the trainers?" Duke asked as they entered the doctor's office.

Mason sighed. He had made the decision last night after Clara left that he was going to find a way to distance himself from her. It was obvious her feelings didn't match his and having her come by every day would just be torture. "Clara is the athletic trainer they assigned me to."

"And? I thought you liked Clara." Duke's eyebrows arched in question.

Mason checked in with the receptionist before answering. "Yeah, I thought things would be okay, but then last night she was at my house, and we kind of had a moment." He sat down in a chair close to the door.

"A moment? What exactly is a moment? I'm afraid I'm going to need a little more information to understand this sudden change of yours."

Mason ran a hand across his neck. "We kissed. It was probably stupid, but she had this smile, and she looked at me like she wanted me to kiss her. You know that look when a woman's eyes focus on your lips?"

Duke chuckled. "Yeah, I know the look. So, what happened?"

Mason shook his head. "Her father called and suddenly she was different. Stiffer. She wouldn't even tell him she was with me."

Duke had met Clara's dad a few times, and Mason had often shared his suspicions of her father's influence, so he was confident Duke understood what that meant. "Did you ask her about it?"

Mason fixed him with a pointed stare. "Of course I did, but she said she didn't actually lie to him, she just didn't volunteer the information. I asked her if her father was the reason we broke up and she denied it." He paused and blew out a frustrated breath. "I just know he had something to do with it."

Duke folded one arm across his chest and propped his chin up with the other. "I know her father wasn't easy on you, but I think you might be making a bit of a jump there. Maybe there's just something going on with her father that you don't know about."

"Like the fact that he doesn't like me for whatever reason and wants to keep us apart?" The sarcasm dripped from Mason's voice.

"Or maybe something else. Look, people withdraw for all sorts of reasons. You remember how sad Dad got when Grandpa died?"

Mason remembered. He had been ten when their grandfather had been killed. Their father had picked them up from school and burst into tears as soon as they got into the car. It had taken nearly ten minutes for him to get the story out, and then Mason and Duke had joined in with the waterworks. What had been odd was that the grandfather had been their mother's father, and she had barely seemed sad at all. At least until a month later when she had completely lost it during a church service.

"Okay, but no one died."

"That you know of. How long has it been since you and Clara really talked?"

Mason opened his mouth to respond but realized Duke was right. They hadn't talked about her family or much of the past six years. "Maybe you're right," he said with a sigh, "but until I know for sure, it just seems safer for my heart to not be too close to her."

"Unless she's the right woman," Duke said, "then doing whatever it takes is worth it. If you don't, you might be pushing away the one woman who can heal your heart."

Mason didn't get a chance to respond as he was called back for his appointment.

"The cast looks good," the doctor said after examining his ankle. "You'll still want to stay off it for a few more days, but we'll get you fitted for a walking boot so you can start putting pressure on it."

"The doctor at the hospital said four to eight weeks of recovery time. Is that about right?"

"I would say that's a fair estimate. We'll leave the cast on for a week and then have you come back. We'll run another scan to see if it's healing, and if it is, then we can start physical therapy."

Mason nodded. It wasn't what he'd hoped to hear but it was what he'd expected. He didn't bother to ask for a new scooter as the one Clara had brought him appeared to be working fine. With his new boot on and adjusted, he headed back out to Duke who'd waited in the reception area.

"All good?" Duke asked as he approached.

"For now. Follow up in five days." Mason patted his shirt pocket which held his release papers and all the instructions for care for the next few days.

Duke nodded. "All right, back home then?"

Mason checked his watch. More than likely Clara had already come and gone, but what if she'd stuck around to wait for his return? Duke's words still tumbled through his mind, but he needed more time to process them. "Actually, can we just drive around for a bit? Maybe grab some lunch?"

Duke shook his head and chuckled. "You're going to have to face her again sooner or later."

"I know, but I'm settling for later right now."

"All right, let's grab some food and then maybe we can work on a plan to get her back. If that's what you want."

20

CLARA

Clara's guilt was still weighing on her as she pulled into Mason's driveway to take him to his appointment. He was right. Her father had been the reason they broke up. Or at least the main part of the reason. He'd offered to pay for Mason's college funds if she broke it off, and Clara had known Mason could use the money. Sure, she could have said no, but it certainly hadn't been her idea to break it off.

He was also right about the current situation. She hadn't told her father about the interview at first because she'd been afraid he would tell her not to go. Then she had deliberately failed to mention the team she worked for was the same one Mason played for. She'd just known he would pressure her to quit. And she couldn't imagine what he would do if he found out she was spending every day with Mason through his recovery. Drag her back to their small town probably, but why was she letting him control her life still?

She was no longer a girl in high school, dependent on her father's money. She had a good job, a steady income, and she could fend for herself no matter what her father said, so why was she so afraid of him? The truth was, she was afraid he would tell Mason. He said he still cared for her, but would he if he knew what she had done?

She couldn't let him know. Yes, this way hurt, but this was her cross to bear for her decision, and whatever pain she caused Mason now was way less than he would suffer if he knew the truth. She just needed to rebuild that wall in her heart and make sure she didn't let it lower again.

Using the front door key felt even more awkward after last night, but she didn't want to make him hobble to the door either. So, she unlocked the door and opened it slightly as she knocked. "Hello, it's Clara. I'm here to take you to your appointment."

Mason was not in the living room, nor did he holler out at the sound of her voice. A tremor of anxiety sprouted in her stomach. Was he injured? Just ignoring her? "Mason?" She continued into the kitchen, but he wasn't there either. However, she did spy a bowl in the sink, so he had been here at some point.

She spun around slowly trying to decide if she should go upstairs and look for him and that's when she saw it. A note propped on the table with her name on it. She walked to the table and picked up the piece of paper, knowing what it said before she even read it.

"Clara, I asked Duke to take me in today. No need to worry about me. I'll call you if I need you. Mason."

So, that was it. He was washing his hands of her. Though she couldn't blame him after the way she'd acted last night, the dismissal hurt. Plus, Justin had assigned her to help him. What was she going to tell him?

"Lord, I messed up," she said softly, "please show me how to fix this."

With no immediate answer and nothing more to do in Mason's house without Mason there, Clara locked up and headed to work. Hopefully, she could avoid Justin.

As she pulled into the parking lot of the facility, her cell phone rang. A sigh escaped her lips as she saw her father's number again. What could he want this time?

"Hey, Dad, what's up?" She tried to make her voice sound more cheerful than she felt.

"I was wondering if you might be free for an early lunch, Clara. I'm in town on a little business today, and I'd like to meet up with you."

Clara bit her lip. Technically, she could probably meet him. Justin wasn't expecting her until later anyway, but what if Mason showed up after his appointment? He probably wouldn't though. She had a feeling he was going to do every-thing he could to avoid her for a while, and if she said no to her father, he would just keep nagging her. "Okay, Dad, I can give you a few hours. Where do you want to meet?"

"There's a nice sit-down restaurant on Baker street isn't there?"

Clara closed her eyes and tried to picture the town. She was still figuring her way around most places, but Baker was one of the streets she was more familiar with. "Do you mean The Oasis Cafe?"

"Yes, that's the place. I'll meet you there at eleven."

Clara glanced at her watch. It was 10:40 now which would give her plenty of time to get there by eleven. "On my way."

She hung up the phone and put the car in reverse. Hopefully this had been the right decision. If nothing else, it would buy her a little time to think of what to tell Justin.

Her father's car was already in the parking lot when she pulled in. At least she wouldn't have to wait for him. She hated being the first one to arrive at places.

As she entered the quaint restaurant, she saw him wave to her from a table near the back. Why had he picked a table for four when it was just the two of them? Or was it just the two of them? There appeared to be three glasses and place settings on the table.

"Clara, so glad you could meet me for lunch," her father said as she pulled the chair out across from him. He was not a hugger, so she wasn't too shocked by his more cordial greeting. Besides, her curiosity was still focused on the extra glass.

"Don't you mean us?" she said, motioning to the other place setting.

A slight pink colored his cheeks, and he cleared his throat. "Ah, yes, I know you've been busy, but I ran into an old friend of mine. He's in town, so I invited him to join us."

"You set me up on a blind date?" Clara could not believe her father. First, he had controlled her relationship with Mason. Then he had pushed her into a relationship with Joel whom she had nothing in common with. Now, he was trying to do it again with some other man?

"It's not a date; it's a lunch, and it's certainly not a blind date. Joel told me you've been ghosting him, so I figured this would allow you to explain why and reconcile."

Ire flared up in Clara. "You invited Joel? Dad, I broke up with him." Or she'd figured that if she stopped calling and returning his calls that he would realize she was breaking up with him. He was, after all, a well-educated man with a brain.

"Funny, it seems you forgot to mention that to him," her father said with a pointed tone, "but no matter. I assured him you had probably just been busy. He's willing to forgive you, and you could do a lot worse than Joel."

The contempt in his voice referred to Mason, and it took all of her control not to lash out at him. She still didn't understand why he hated Mason so much. So, he hadn't been as wealthy as them growing up, he was certainly doing well for himself now. And how could her father just assume she would get back together with Joel because he brought him? And make up an excuse for her? The nerve of this man was incredible.

Clara opened her mouth to tell him she was not interested in dating anyone, especially someone that he picked for her, but the appearance of a man in a tailored suit pulling out the chair next to her father stopped her.

"Ah, here he is now. Joel, so good to see you again. It seems Clara was finally able to break free from her busy job to join us."

"Is that why you can't pick up a phone?" Joel asked as he sat down.

Clara bit her lip to hold back her equally snide response. Her father had pushed her into dating Joel, but now that she really looked at him, she couldn't believe she had ever agreed to date him. It wasn't that he wasn't nice looking; he certainly had been blessed in that area with his dark hair and deep blue eyes, but he was too stiff for Clara's taste. His suit looked expensive, Armani probably, but that was no surprise. Her father certainly wouldn't set her up with anyone who didn't have money. His dark hair was cut close to his head, with every hair seeming to lay in the right place. She doubted he ever left his house with a hair out of place. However, it was his hands that really got her. Not only were they soft as if they never saw hard work, but she was convinced his nails looked more manicured than hers.

"I figured you were smart enough to get my hint." Clara smiled as she said the words as if that might diffuse the sting a little.

"Clara, that is no way to talk to Joel," her father barked.

"Well, I wasn't expecting Joel, Dad," she said pointedly at him. "I agreed to have lunch with you. When you surprise me with unexpected guests, you get unexpected reactions."

The glare he shot her was fiercer than she had seen in a long time, but she wasn't backing down. Not this time. This time she was standing up for herself as she should have done six years ago and several times since. This was going to be a long lunch.

21

MASON

Mason couldn't believe he was going to have to watch this game from the sidelines. He was grateful they had advanced, but not being able to play was excruciating. Almost as hard as seeing Clara. He hadn't spoken to her since the botched movie night, but he assumed she had filled Justin in on the situation because Davis, the other offensive trainer, had checked in with him a few times over the last few days. Over the phone and not in person, but at least he hadn't had to deal with Clara. Yet.

"You going to be okay over here?" Blaine asked as he spun a football in his hands. It was almost time for warm ups, and Mason appreciated the gesture of his captain stopping by to check on him. Blaine hadn't been the only teammate. It seemed almost everyone had wanted to see how he was doing on the flight over.

Mason shrugged. "Not my favorite place to watch a game, but I'm glad to be here."

Blaine nodded as if he understood the feeling. "It wouldn't be a game without you. Look, I know this is hard, but you cheer for us the same as you would if you were playing. That energy will carry us forward, and we'll take home that championship ring again this year."

"Yeah, sounds good, man." Mason had been trying to make peace with the fact that he wouldn't play the rest of this season, but it was still hard. Add that to the night he'd had with Clara, and it had been a rough week for sure.

A whistle sounded, and Blaine flashed a wave before heading out onto the field for warmups. Mason sat down on the sideline bench and stretched his ankle out. The pain was diminishing, but it still screamed at him when he spent too much time on it.

"Is this seat taken?"

Mason looked up to see Clara standing at the edge of the bench. He shrugged and scooted over to make room for her. Though he still wasn't sure how he felt about her at the moment, Duke's words reminded him that he shouldn't judge until he had all the facts.

"I wanted to apologize to you," she said, running her hands down her thighs. "I should have told my dad I was with you."

"So, why didn't you?"

Clara took a deep breath. "My dad has controlled my life

for a long time. He wasn't always that way, but when my mom died, he became super protective."

Mason scoffed. Super protective was not the word he would use to describe her father. Insolent and overbearing seemed like much better adjectives.

Clara offered a small smile. "Anyway, part of why I took this job was to get out from under my father's thumb, but I guess some habits die hard. I was afraid if he knew that I was working on your team or with you that he might try to make me go back to the University of Texas."

"Why does your father hate me so much?" He watched as Clara sighed and tucked a strand of her hair behind her ears.

"I don't think he hates you, Mason. He just never thought you were good enough for me."

"Ouch." Though Mason had figured that was the reason, hearing her say it still hurt.

"The thing is…" She turned to him, looking him in the eyes for the first time since she sat down. "He's wrong. You are good enough for me. Maybe too good for me."

Too good for her? "What do you mean?"

"Clara, it's time to get set up," Justin's voice called from over her shoulder.

"Let's do dinner later, and I'll tell you everything, okay?"

He wanted to ask more questions, to demand that she stay and explain what she meant, but he could see the pleading in her eyes as well as Justin's impatient stance a few feet away. "Okay, dinner."

"Thank you." She squeezed his arm and flashed a small smile before darting off to help Justin and Davis finish setting up.

Mason watched her, wondering what she wanted to tell him. Perhaps this was good though. It would give him time to sort out his own thoughts before they had a heart to heart conversation.

MASON GRIPPED THE EDGE OF THE BENCH AS THE TWO-minute buzzer went off. This game had been another close one, and the Tornadoes were only up by three points. A field goal from the other team would tie the game, and a touch-down would mean the Tornadoes were done. He wasn't sure if it was because he wasn't playing or because it was now up to the defense, but Mason had never felt so stressed in a game.

The offensive line including Blaine, Tucker, and Jefferson paced around near him. They too could do nothing unless the other team lost the ball, and he realized they must feel as helpless as he did. At least for the moment.

The two-minute warning ended, and the defensive line jogged back out onto the field. It was first and ten, and their job was to keep the other side from advancing down the field or scoring.

The crowd noise was so deafening that Mason couldn't

even hear the count from his position on the field, but he saw the ball go flying through the air. He held his breath, hoping the receiver would miss, but the ball landed perfectly in his arms, and though he was tackled immediately, the other team had just gained another eight yards. A few more yards would put them into field goal range.

A blocked run was the next play, and Mason's heartbeat thundered in his ears. Third and two wasn't much, but if the defense could hold them, it might be the end of the game. Of course, there was a chance the other team would attempt a field goal kick even if they were slightly out of range as a last resort. He'd seen miracle kicks win games before.

The third down play ended with a dropped ball, and Mason held his breath. This was the moment of truth. Either the team would try to get the two yards, or they would attempt a field goal kick. He hoped they would go for the latter. The chances a kicker would miss from this far out was better than the chance they wouldn't get the two yards. He held his breath, waiting to see what they'd choose.

He sighed when the kicker remained on the sidelines. His hand ran across the back of his neck as he watched the teams line up again. Having expected a run, he was surprised when the ball flew through the air. Surprise turned to disappointment as the ball was caught well within field goal range. The clock was still ticking though. Only a minute to go.

After a rushed lineup, the quarterback spiked the ball bringing the downs to second and ten with fifty seconds left on the clock. Plenty of time if the defense didn't do their job. Mason felt like his heart was being squeezed by a giant vise. He always felt excitement during games, but sitting here watching seemed more nerve-wracking than normal.

The third down play resulted in no gain, and this time the kicker did come out on the field. A forty-five-yard field goal wasn't a shoo-in, but it was well within this kicker's range. Mason bit down on the knuckle of his index finger as the kicker lined up. This could go two ways. Either he made it, and the game went into overtime, or he missed and the Tornadoes moved on.

The clock continued counting down, and the ball was snapped. The kicker's form appeared perfect as the ball went sailing through the air. Mason followed it with his eyes, feeling like he was watching it spiral and spin in slow motion as it headed for the goal posts. It was a little far to the right, but when it landed on the other side, Mason couldn't tell if it had been good or just outside the posts. He turned to look at the large screen for a replay and nearly jumped to his feet when he saw the ball was outside the posts.

A massive cheer went up around him as the players high fived and clapped shoulders. They had done it. They'd made it to the championship game again. Though Mason was happy for the win, he still felt the sting of disappointment. He'd be watching the championship game from the sidelines this year instead of playing.

"We did it," Jefferson said, coming up to him.

"You did. Great game." Mason forced a smile to his face. It wasn't Jefferson's fault that he didn't get to play. No, that was his fault and his alone.

Jefferson's smile faded into an expression of understanding. "I know it's hard not playing, but believe me there are worse things than missing a game." His eyes took on a sadness that didn't normally reside there, and Mason wondered what was hiding in Jefferson's past.

Just as quickly, his eyes brightened and he clapped Mason on the shoulder. "Besides, I learned almost everything I know from you, so it's like you were out there. In spirit at least."

"Almost, huh?" Mason knew Jefferson was trying to make him feel better, and he appreciated the gesture.

Jefferson shrugged and flashed a teasing grin. "I did know some things before I met you. Had to get on the team somehow, right?"

His comical expression made Mason chuckle, and the cloud of sadness receded a little bit. He did have a lot to be thankful for, including his dinner with Clara later that hopefully would reveal if a future romance between the two of them had a chance.

22

CLARA

Clara caught Mason's eye as they got off the shuttle back at the Tornado complex. It was late, and the team had grabbed dinner on the way, but she still felt the need to talk to him. After the coerced lunch date with Joel, she had decided it was time to tell Mason everything. It might ruin their chances of a future relationship, but at least she would feel better knowing he knew the truth.

"So, dinner didn't work out, but do you still feel like hearing what I have to say?" she asked as she slowed her step to match his slower pace.

"Of course," he said with a slight grin. "I've been on pins and needles all day."

Clara swatted his arm. While she had no doubt he was curious as to what she had eluded to, his response was grossly exaggerated. "I'm sure you have. Did someone drive you here?"

"I certainly didn't drive myself," he said, pointing down at his booted ankle. He was still on the crutches though she had seen him place a little weight on the foot throughout the day. "Duke dropped me off."

"Well, how about I drive you home and we can talk there?"

"Lead the way," he said, motioning with his arm.

Clara tried to formulate the words in her head as she drove, but nothing sounded right. They were still a jumbled mess when she pulled into Mason's driveway, and she had no idea how he was going to react. After helping him out of the car, she followed him up the entrance and into his house.

"Living room?" Mason asked as he shut the door behind them.

"Sure, that will be fine." Clara took a deep breath as she sat on the couch. She stared down at her hands, collecting her thoughts before glancing up at Mason. "So, I haven't been completely honest with you."

His brow lifted as he cocked his head at her. "Okay, what haven't you been honest about?"

"About why we broke up back in high school."

Mason leaned forward, an intensity flowing from his eyes. "I knew it. Your father was involved, wasn't he?"

Clara bit her lip and nodded. "He was, but so were yours."

"What?" Disbelief colored his voice and his expression.

"My father didn't think you were good enough for me. To be honest, I don't think he ever thought you'd become a pro player. I'd love for him to see you now." She shook her head to rein in her train of thought. "Anyway, he reached out to your parents with his concerns. Evidently, they had some about me. They thought I would distract you and keep you from making pro, so they came up with an agreement."

"What agreement?" Mason's voice was ice cold.

"He offered to pay for your college if we broke up." She paused and took another deep breath. "They accepted and he brought the offer to me. I didn't want to take it, Mason, but I knew college was important for you. You needed to be on a college team to get discovered by the draft. I also knew your parents couldn't really afford to send both you and Duke at the same time. I know it was wrong, but I thought I was doing the best thing I could for you."

"The best thing for me?" Mason's eyes grew to the size of quarters as his voice rose in pitch. "How was that the best thing for me? You were the best thing that ever happened to me, Clara. I thought I was going to marry you, and I've struggled to have a real relationship since because I never understood what went wrong."

She blinked at him, trying to make sense of his words. He'd thrown a lot at her, but only a few were sticking in her mind. "Wait, you were going to marry me?"

Mason scoffed and shook his head. "Yeah, I had a ring

picked out and everything."

Tears filled Clara's eyes. He had loved her as much as she had loved him, and she had messed it up. How could she have been so stupid to listen to her father. "Mason, I'm so sorry."

"Me too," he said with a sigh and then ran his hand through his hair.

"Do you think?" The words stuck in her throat. "Do you think we can get past this and try again? I may have let you go, but I never stopped loving you."

Mason's jaw clenched, and his hand slid down his cheek. "I don't know, Clara. Why did you decide to tell me this now anyway?"

A mirthless chuckle escaped Clara's mouth. She might as well tell him everything. Go big or go home, right? "My father called me on Tuesday when you went to your appointment without me. He invited me to lunch. Only when I got there, he had invited this guy Joel I was seeing before I took the job here." Mason's brow furrowed and she knew he was about to ask what this had to do with anything, so she hurried on. "I didn't care for Joel. I was dating him because my father pushed us together, but when he blindsided me like that, I realized he was never going to let me live my life if I didn't stand up to him."

"And did you? Stand up to him?"

Clara's mind flashed back to the encounter. Though not her finest hour, she had definitely stood up to him. "I did. I think you would have been proud of me. He wasn't pleased, but I told Joel I wasn't interested in him, and then I told my father to stop running my life. When I left the restaurant, I felt like I was on cloud nine, like I could do anything. Still, this dark spot hung over me. The past between us. As much as I was afraid it might drive you away, I knew I needed to tell you the whole truth."

"I'm glad you finally did," Mason said, and he sounded sincere, but Clara wanted more than his forgiveness. She wanted to know if their future had a chance. "And I know you want to know if this means we can have a chance again, but this is a lot to take in. I need a little processing time."

"Of course. I'm sorry." It wasn't what she wanted to hear, but she could understand his feelings. She had just dropped quite the bomb on him. She grabbed her purse and stood. "I guess I'll see you later?"

"Yeah, later." His tone was noncommittal and cold, and it broke Clara's heart.

She had suspected he would be angry with her, but she had hoped he would understand the position she had been placed in and forgive her. Perhaps she shouldn't have told him. She could have taken the secret to her grave. No. She shook her head. If she wanted a chance at a real relationship with him, then she had to be honest. Otherwise her father probably would have told him at some inopportune moment and ruined everything anyway. It was better this way, even if he never forgave her.

A tear slid down her cheek as she climbed into her car. She'd been so certain he would be happy he'd been right all these years that he would take her in his arms and rekindle their relationship with a searing kiss, but she should have known better. Things never worked out that nicely for her. Now, she had pushed her father away and possibly Mason too. Could this night get any worse?

She backed out of his driveway and wiped a tear with her hand. How was she going to continue working with him if he didn't forgive her? He would have to. She had felt such peace that telling him was the right thing that she couldn't believe God would have steered her wrong. He just needed time like he said.

Clara sniffed back another tear as the sign for the interstate appeared. Normally, she would avoid the interstate, but at this time of night, the traffic would be light, and she would probably get home quicker. She was fairly certain a tub of half-eaten ice cream would be waiting for her in her freezer so she could drown out her sorrows with its creamy goodness.

She signaled her turn onto the interstate, and then glanced over her shoulder to make sure she was free to merge. The sound of horns registered moments before the bright lights. Clara turned just in time to see a truck going the wrong way slam into the front of her car. There was a loud pop and then the world went dark.

23

MASON

Mason checked the time again. Duke was late. He knew he was asking a lot of his brother to take him to yet another appointment, but he hoped the doctor would remove the ankle cast today and let him start physical therapy. Then maybe he could start driving himself places and stop inconveniencing his brother.

Of course he could have asked Clara, but after the bombshell she'd dropped last night, he wasn't ready to see her yet. Though he'd expected her father had played a hand in their breakup, hearing her admit she had allowed it so he could go to college still stung. Yes, money had been tight for him then, but he would have found a way to do it without her father's money. If only she had cared about him enough to tell him. And that was the issue he couldn't get past. If she had cared about him as much as she said she had, why not come to him and tell him her father's plan? How could he trust her to be honest with him in the future?

In fact, how could he trust his parents? They'd also lied to him and conspired to separate him from Clara. He would have to confront them about that soon as well.

The knock on his door came just as he was checking the time again. Finally. He hobbled to the door and opened it to an apologetic Duke on the other side.

"Sorry man, traffic was a nightmare."

"It's okay, but we better hurry up or we'll be late." Mason locked the door behind him and followed Duke to his truck. It took him a minute to get into the truck and sit comfortably, but soon Duke was tearing down the road. Mason knew he should tell him to slow down, but he enjoyed watching the scenery fly by. The jumbled images matched his mood.

"So, you want to tell me what's got you so pensive?" Duke asked after they had been driving nearly ten minutes in silence. "And don't tell me it's about me being late because we'll be there in plenty of time."

"No, it's not about that. Clara came over last night to tell me something, and it kind of rocked my world." He turned from gazing out the window to regard his brother. "Did you know Mom and Dad conspired with her father to break us up?"

Duke's eyebrow lifted, and he shook his head. "No, but what do you mean conspire?"

"Did you know my scholarship money wasn't really a scholarship?" Mason pressed, ignoring Duke's question.

"No, what are you talking about man? You aren't making any sense." Duke glanced at him, his brow furrowed in confusion, before turning his attention back to the road.

"Clara's dad paid for my college. Mom and Dad told me it was a scholarship, but it wasn't. How could they do that, Duke?"

"I always thought someone paying for your college was a good thing," Duke said.

"Not if there's a condition attached that says the only way I get it is if Clara breaks up with me."

Duke let out a low whistle. "That's what she told you happened?"

Mason ran a frustrated hand across his forehead. "Yeah, and now I don't know what to do with that information. I'm mad at Clara for letting her father tear us apart and for not talking to me. I'm mad at her father for making the offer. I'm mad at Mom and Dad for taking it, and I'm mad at the six years I lost with her."

"That's a lot of anger," Duke said as he pulled into a parking space. He turned off the engine and faced Mason. "I'm not saying you don't have a right to be angry because you do, but maybe it's time you did some soul searching about what's really important."

"What do you mean?" Mason asked.

"Well, it appears to me that God may have brought the

woman you loved back into your life, and if she finally told you what happened back in high school, then maybe she's now in a position to make a different choice. The right choice. As for Mom and Dad, yeah you should talk to them, but they wanted to give you a chance. Should they have taken that deal? No, at least not without talking to you, but I honestly think they had your best interests at heart."

Mason bit his lip as he thought about Duke's words. Maybe he was right. How many players did he know who were still dating their high school girlfriends? None. In fact, he could count on one hand the number of people he knew who married their high school sweethearts. Would he and Clara have ended up the same way if they had stayed together?

And Duke was right about her being in a new place. That was evident not only from her ability to tell him about the past but also from the extra information she gave about standing up to her father. A relationship with her while her father still hated him would be hard, but if she was able to stand up to him now, it would at least be possible.

And then there were his parents. He wasn't a father yet, but he imagined he would be tempted to take an offer like that for his own kid if he knew it was the only way to help them succeed. Heck, it was the plot line of half the movies he watched - parents doing terrible things to save their children. It didn't make it right, but it was believable.

Had God really arranged for all of this to happen so that

he and Clara could have a second chance when they both
might be ready for one? It was certainly an interesting
thought to consider.

"You speak wise words, my brother," Mason finally said.

Duke shrugged. "Eh, with age comes wisdom."

Mason chuckled. "Hah. If you're so wise, then how come
you haven't found a woman and settled down yet?"

"Who says I haven't?" Duke said as he opened his door
and stepped out.

"Wait, what?" Mason flung his door open and nearly lost
his crutches in his hurry to catch up with his brother. "You
can't drop a bombshell like that and just walk away."

"Actually, I can," Duke said with a laugh. "I still have
two working feet."

Mason struggled to keep up with Duke. He wasn't sure if
his brother was being serious or just trying to lighten the
mood, but he was determined to hear about this girl if she
existed.

24

CLARA

"Clara, can you hear me?"

Clara blinked and tried to focus on Mason's voice. It was Mason, wasn't it? He sounded so far off though, and her eyes felt so heavy.

"Clara, I'm here."

She felt his hand grab hers, and she struggled to open her eyes. Where was she? A soft, beeping noise joined Mason's voice, and there was a constant hum that she couldn't place. Definitely not her apartment, but then where? And then the image of the bright headlights filled her mind. Her eyes flashed open as she gasped and then grimaced in pain.

"Clara? Are you okay?"

Clara took a moment to assess her pain before answering. "I think so, but my chest really hurts as does my head. What time is it?" She turned her head slowly to regard Mason. He sat in a chair at her bedside, concern covering his handsome features.

"Noon. You've been out for a while according to the nurse. I guess you suffered a concussion as well as bruised ribs in the accident."

"That would explain why everything feels hazy, but what are you doing here? I thought you needed time."

The corners of his lips pulled into a smile. "I thought I did too, but it's amazing how that view changes when you find out someone you love has been injured." He squeezed her hand a little tighter.

Someone you love. The words were so sweet to her ears. She had thought perhaps she had destroyed their chance last night, but something had obviously changed his mind. She was curious as to what. "I love you too though this isn't how I pictured telling you." She chuckled slightly and then grimaced in pain again.

"It doesn't matter how you tell me." His smile widened. "I'm just happy to hear it."

She squeezed his hand with as much strength as she could muster. "I'm happy to hear it and say it too, but how did you even find out I was here?"

Mason chuckled. "That's kind of a long story. When Duke picked me up for my appointment this morning, I was still angry at everything, but he showed me how the timing of this might have been God's timing. I thought about that during my appointment and decided that he was right. So, I tried calling you. At first no one picked up, but finally a nurse answered and told me what had happened. I came right over."

Clara smiled at him. "That wasn't a very long story."

A deep, warm laugh tumbled out of Mason's lips, and his eyes twinkled. "Yeah, I guess not the way I told it. It felt a lot longer, but that was probably due to my inner turmoil."

"I can see that." She was glad to see the concern leave his face. "How did your appointment go by the way?"

"It went well. The doctor removed the cast and told me to start putting weight on it. No more crutches. Of course it means I'm even slower now."

"You'll probably be faster than me." Clara tried not to chuckle to avoid the crushing pain on her chest. "At least for a little while."

"I have no doubt you'll rebound sooner though. I guess we'll both be taking it easy at the championship game."

"But at least we'll be doing it together," she said softly.

A knock sounded at the hospital door, and Clara glanced over to see Duke enter.

"Hope I'm not intruding, but we wanted to give you these." He held up a beautiful vase of flowers and balloons that read "Get Well Soon."

It had been ages since Clara had seen Duke, but she'd

always liked Mason's older brother. He'd never treated the two of them like they were annoyances even though they were two years younger. Instead, he'd driven them places before they had their licenses and continued to hang out with them often when they had movie nights at the Dixon's house.

"Thank you, Duke. That is so thoughtful."

"Well, it was Mason's idea. I just did the purchasing and delivering because otherwise we still wouldn't have made it to the gift shop yet." He held his hand up as if whispering an aside. "In case you haven't noticed, he's a little slow these days."

Mason shot his brother a glare. "You just wait until my tendon heals, and then we'll see who the slow one is."

Duke set the flowers down and then held his hands up in defense. "No argument from me, little brother. You've always been faster which is why you're the athlete and I'm the advertiser."

Clara smiled as she watched the two bicker the same way they used to in high school. She supposed sibling rivalries didn't change much even over the years.

"I don't mean to break up this family quarrel, but has a doctor been in? Do you know when I might get out of here?" Clara knew her recovery would not be immediate, but she'd certainly rather recoup in her own house where she could curl up in her warm jammies and binge watch her favorite shows.

Mason shook his head. "I haven't seen one yet."

"I'll go see if I can track one down," Duke said, before ducking out of the room.

"Thank you for coming, Mason."

"You're welcome, but you know we're going to have to talk to my parents and your father, right?"

The sigh that escaped Clara seemed to hold the weight of the world. She knew he was right, but she certainly wasn't excited about the prospect of it. Things were already rocky with her father after the botched lunch, and she didn't look forward to upsetting his parents as well. Still, though they were adults, their relationship would be better if they could get the blessings of their families.

"I know, but maybe that can wait until I can breathe a little easier?"

"I think we can make that happen," Mason said with a reassuring smile.

"I hear we're awake and itching to go home," an unfamiliar female voice said from the doorway.

Clara looked up to see a woman in a white coat enter the room. She grabbed the chart by the door and scanned it. "How is the pain, Ms. Bradford?"

"Manageable," Clara said. "My head is pounding a little and my chest hurts, but if there's nothing more serious, I'm ready to go home."

"You have some internal bruising, but other than your concussion, your injuries are actually pretty minor. You were lucky, Ms. Bradford. It appears someone was watching out for you. I'd like to do a final check and then I'll sign your release papers. Be back in a bit."

"Thank you," Clara said before smiling back at Mason. He'd suggested their reunion was due to God's timing, and she was pretty certain her non-serious injuries were as well. It might have been a rough six years, but it looked as if God was blessing them even more because of it.

25

MASON

Mason's heart thudded in his chest as he checked the time again. It was Friday evening, four days since Clara's injury, and the night he and Clara had decided to tell their parents about their rekindled relationship. They'd agreed to use his house since it was bigger and so her father could see how well he was doing.

"It will be okay," she said, coming up beside him and putting her arm through his. "The worst that will happen is that we have to kick them out." She issued an encouraging smile, and he patted her arm.

While she was still sore, she was certainly moving around much better. They'd even gone earlier to get her a rental car while her insurance company worked to get a refund issued to her for the loss of her car due to the accident. He was moving better as well, but the two of them certainly made a humorous pair with his limping gait and her grimace of pain every time she laughed.

"Let's hope it doesn't come to that," he said just as the doorbell rang. He took a deep breath and pulled his shoulders back before stepping away from her and to the door. "Well, here we go."

Mason opened the door to reveal his parents on the other side.

"Mason," his mother said, rushing forward to pull him into a hug. If she saw Clara, it didn't register at first. His father, however, clenched his jaw as he spied her.

"What is this?" he asked, and the tone of his voice caused his mother to pull back and realize Mason was not alone.

"What do you mean?" Mason asked sweetly. "This is me inviting you to dinner to meet my girlfriend." He held out his hand to Clara and pulled her close to him when she placed her hand in his.

"Girlfriend?" His mother's hands flew to her mouth, and her wide eyes jumped between Mason and her husband. "But, that's not possible."

"You mean because you tried to keep us apart?" Mason was surprised at how calm and collected his voice sounded.

His father opened his mouth as if he was going to protest and then sighed. "It wasn't our idea."

"But you still took the money," Mason said. "I can't believe you two would do that."

"She's just as guilty," his mother said in a small voice. "She agreed to break up with you."

"You're right; she did, but she was seventeen and under the rule of her father. You two don't have an excuse."

"We just wanted the best for you," his mother sobbed.

"What is this?" The deep, demanding voice of Clara's father carried over the heads of Mason's parents.

"So glad you could join us, Dad," Clara said, speaking up for the first time. "Why don't you all come inside?"

Though it was evident from the expressions on their faces that coming inside was the last thing they wanted to do, they followed Clara into the living room and took a seat. His parents took the couch while her father took the chair farthest away. Mason almost chuckled at the hostility that still appeared to exist between them.

"I'm going to ask you again, Clara, what is this?"

Clara stepped closer to Mason and stared evenly at her father. "This is me finally standing up for what I want, Dad. The job I took in Southlake is for the Texas Tornadoes, the same team that Mason plays for. Though you tried to tear us apart six years ago, God brought us back together. I know you thought you were doing what was best for me." She turned to look at his parents. "You all did, but you were wrong. Mason and I belong together, and while we hope you will accept our decision and put the past wrongs behind us, we will not be torn apart by you again."

"You can't do this," her father said. "You're supposed to marry Joel, not a… a football player."

"I don't love Joel, Dad. I never did. I love Mason, and I have since high school. I tried to put him out of my mind and do what you wanted, but I was miserable. I applied for the job to get away from you, to get away from Joel. I want you in my life, but you can't run it any longer."

"The same goes for you two," Mason piped up, eyeing his parents. "I understand why you did what you did, but that doesn't make it right. Clara and I want a life with you in it, but only if you accept that what you did was wrong and promise never to try and tear us apart again."

Silence filled the room as eyes exchanged glances. Mason tightened his grip on Clara and forced himself to wait.

"You're right," his father said, finally breaking the silence. "We were wrong. Though we only wanted the best for you, we should have talked to you about it instead of conspiring behind your back." He turned to Clara. "I hope you know that it wasn't that we didn't like you; we just didn't want anything to distract Mason from going pro."

"Thank you, sir," Clara said.

Her father cleared his throat. "I'm sorry too. After your mother died, I just wanted the best for you, and I never thought Mason would make it to a point where he'd be able to take care of you." He turned to Mason. "I'm man enough to admit when I'm wrong. You've definitely defied the odds, and while I would prefer my daughter fall for someone with a more stable career, I won't hold her back from pursuing her dreams any longer."

Mason nodded though inside his heart was bursting with joy. He hadn't been sure what to expect when they'd planned this whole thing, but he should have known that if God could bring him and Clara together after so long, that He could thaw frozen hearts as well. After all, mending relationships was a big part of who He was.

"I'm so glad to hear you say that, Dad," Clara said with a smile. "Well, since we've all decided to try being friends, who would like to join us for dinner?"

❦ 26 ❦

CLARA

C lara smiled over at Mason as he leaned forward in anticipation. Though she knew he would rather be out playing the game, he had managed to make peace with his situation and instead had thrown his energy into healing and recovering as quickly as possible.

She was almost entirely healed. While deep coughs or laughing fits still sent her hand to her chest every now and then, for the most part, she was back to normal and back to work. Justin had been kind enough to give her the whole week after the accident off, and she and Mason had spent every day together. It was amazing how they'd been able to pick back up almost as if they had never broken up.

"I see things are going well," Davis said from beside her.

Heat flared across her cheeks as she turned to face him. "What do you mean?" They hadn't really disclosed their relationship to anyone on the team yet, deciding to wait until the championship game was over in case it meant she had to find another job.

"I saw it in your eyes the first time you looked at him and the day he was injured. That's the same way my wife looks at me."

Clara glanced quickly over at Justin to make sure he was out of earshot. "We didn't mean for it to happen, but we dated in high school. While we both thought that had been our chance, it seems God had something more planned."

"He always does," Davis said and flashed a small wink.

"Do you know if there's anything in the contract about dating? We had planned to talk to Justin and the coach tomorrow and disclose."

Davis ran a hand across his chin. "I don't know, but these are good people, and they would be silly to lose either of you. It might mean you get reassigned to defense, but I doubt you'll have much to worry about."

Clara smiled and squeezed Davis's arm. "Thank you. You've been a great friend, and I'm so glad I've gotten to know and work with you." Clara had worked with a lot of male trainers in her time and they generally fell into two categories: the ones who hated her because she was a woman or the ones who ignored her because they thought she couldn't do the job as well. She'd met very few who actually treated her like an equal and it was refreshing. The fact that Davis was a fellow believer only made it even better.

She turned her attention back to the game and grinned as Mason shot to his feet and cheered as Jefferson made an impressive reception. She had no idea what the future held for his injury, but she was glad to see him cheering his teammates on.

As the two-minute warning sounded, Clara moved to stand by Mason. The Tornadoes were down by seven and a hail Mary pass was the only real option they had. She knew it had to bother him that he wasn't out there, fighting for his place on the field and his opportunity to score.

The ball snapped and Blaine sent it flying down the field. Jefferson jumped up, but the defender managed to get in front of the ball and sent it careening in the other direction and away from any Tornado receiver. A silence fell in the stadium as the referees whistled the ball dead. That was it. The Tornadoes had lost.

Clara bit her lip as she waited to see how Mason would react. "Mason, I'm so sorry."

He looked up at her and shook his head. "Don't be. The team played hard, and they wouldn't have been any better with me out there." His shoulders lifted in a small shrug. "Besides, we won last year. We can't win every year. I'll be right back."

Clara smiled as she watched him hobble out to congratulate his team members. God had really been working on his heart, and it was amazing to see. After slapping hands and having an extra-long talk with Jefferson, Mason made his way back to her.

"You really are amazing, you know that?" she said when he was within ear shot.

"Nah, I just realized the last few weeks what's really important. Games are great and winning is awesome, don't get me wrong, but having you back in my life is even better."

Tears filled Clara's eyes. She felt the same way, but it was so nice to hear him say it.

"In fact, I can think of only one thing that would make this day better," he continued.

"A healed tendon?" Clara ventured, her voice still choked with emotion.

"Nope, you agreeing to be my wife." Mason pulled a box out of his pocket and slowly lowered to one knee. "I've had this ring for six years, Clara, and I can't wait any longer to give it to you." He opened the box and stared up at her. "Will you make me the happiest man on earth and marry me?"

"Yes!" The tears she had been trying to hold back spilled down her cheeks and without caring who saw, she dropped to her knees as well. He slid the ring on her finger and then her hands were on his cheeks. Electricity zinged between them and the world around them faded away. "I love you, Mason Dixon," she said before leaning forward and touching her lips to his.

She had no idea how long the kiss lasted, but the deafening sound of cheers and clapping finally registered in her brain and she pulled back, embarrassed that everyone on the team now seemed to be watching them. She scanned the faces to see if the coach or Justin was angry, but everyone was smiling down at them.

"Bout time you joined the club," Tucker said, helping Mason to his feet. "I'm pretty sure you couldn't have chosen a better woman."

Clara's face heated again as players and coaches issued their congratulations.

Blaine held up his hands to quiet the noise. "We played hard today, and while we might have come up short, it appears we still have a reason to celebrate. Who's with me?"

The crowd around them cheered again, and Mason pulled her to his chest. Though it was noisy and crowded and Clara could hardly hear herself think, she decided there was no place she'd rather be. In the short time she'd been with this team, they had become like family to her, and she could only hope she'd have several more years with them in the future.

EPILOGUE

Mason stared at the room in amazement. The team had wanted to do something special for him, and so they had hosted his rehearsal dinner at the team facility. However, it didn't look like the normal cafeteria. Instead, some of the tables had been cleared and ribbons and flowers had been hung around the room. At the front, several tables had been placed together to hold the array of food that had been provided.

Mason smiled as Clara's eyes grew wide at the table of food laid out for them. "The Tornado chef did all of this?"

"Well, not by herself, but with her team, yeah. The team decided that we needed a proper rehearsal dinner, and they asked her to prepare the food. It's good, right?" Mason could hardly believe the spread himself. There were three entree types, two different salads, a variety of fruits and vegetables, and a plate of the most tantalizing bread he had ever seen.

Clara nodded. "It's amazing. If it tastes half as good as it looks, then I have a feeling I will be leaving stuffed."

Mason chuckled. "You will definitely be leaving stuffed. This chef is amazing." In fact, the new chef was what made summer training worth looking forward to. Last summer had been her first year, and Mason couldn't wait for training to start up again in a few weeks to get more of her delicious food.

"I can't believe the team did all of this for us."

"Believe it," Blaine said, appearing behind them with his new wife, Kenzi. They had married in April, and from the smile on Blaine's face, married life agreed with him. "This team is about family, and you both are an important part. It will be good to have you playing again this year, Mason."

Mason nodded and clapped Blaine on the shoulder. It had taken him until the end of March, but he'd been given a clean bill of health and the green light to resume practice and training. Though he'd put on a few pounds, he had no doubt he would lose it all in the summer heat and come back just as lean as before.

"Thank you for agreeing to be one of my groomsmen," Mason said. Duke was his best man, of course, but thankfully Blaine, Tucker, and Jefferson had agreed to stand with him as well. He wondered briefly where the others were. Other than his parents and Clara's father, Blaine was the first to arrive.

"Wouldn't have missed it for the world. We'll let you continue to greet guests. Those seats near the table are calling our names." Blaine headed off with Kenzi but before Mason could say anything else, Tucker and Shelby walked in. Duke came in next with a pretty blonde Mason had never met before.

"You must be the mystery woman who has charmed my brother," Mason said, sticking out his hand and enjoying the blush that spread across Duke's face.

"Is that what he's calling me?" She looked up at Duke with a teasing smile but eyes that were already cloudy with affection. Mason would have to get the rest of this story later because Duke had obviously been seeing this woman for some time.

"That's not what I called you." Duke shot Mason a burning stare.

The woman just laughed and turned back to Mason and Clara. "I'm Katrina, and you must be Mason and Clara. I hope we'll become good friends."

Mason had no doubt they would if his brother kept her around long enough. Katrina had spunk and Duke needed someone like that in his life.

Adrienne and her husband hurried in shortly after. Mason had never met Adrienne, but he would have recognized her from Clara's description. The woman could have been the Barbie doll model with her blonde hair, blue eyes, and perfect figure. Plus, her dress was starched so stiffly that it flared out around her legs.

"I'm so sorry we're late. The babysitter was running behind, and I didn't think you wanted us to bring the kids." Her eyes widened as she scanned the room. "By the way, this place is amazing."

"It's not a big deal," Clara said, leaning forward to hug the woman. "We're still missing a few people, but I'd love for you to meet Mason."

Adrienne extended her hand, and Mason was surprised by how strong her grip was. She might have been little, but someone had taught her the benefit of a firm handshake.

"It's so nice to meet you. This is my husband, David."

The group shook hands and then Adrienne and David moved off to sit down as well.

Stacy and two other friends from Clara's previous work came in, and then she turned to him. "Is that everyone?"

Mason scanned the room. "Everyone except Jefferson. I wonder where he is."

Clara glanced down at her watch. "Let's give him a few more minutes, and then we'll have to get started."

He knew she was right, but he hoped the young wide receiver made it. They'd become closer in the last few months after his injury, and while he enjoyed the man's company immensely, Mason had begun to think Jefferson might be hiding something.

At that moment, Jefferson flew in the door, looking

flushed and harried.

"Hey, man, glad you could make it. Everything okay?"

Jefferson took a moment to breathe and regain his composure. "Yeah, I just... had something I had to deal with at home."

Mason wanted to pry further, but at that moment, a bell at the front of the room began ringing. "Looks like you're next to us," he whispered as he led the way to the remaining three empty seats.

The bell stopped and Mason looked around to see what was happening next. Suddenly, the head coach walked out from the side door. Mason's eyes widened at the sight of the man in a suit and tie. "I'm so glad you could all make it tonight. As you know, we are here to celebrate Mason's last night of freedom."

Laughter erupted around the room, and the coach smiled at Clara. "I'm just kidding. We all know that Mason is getting the better end of this deal. Clara, though you've only been with us for six months, you've become an important member of this team, and we're so glad that you've decided to continue with us."

"Hear, hear," Blaine added, lifting his glass in the air.

"That's why we wanted to throw this rehearsal dinner for you both, to say thank you for all that you've done. Now, some of you have tasted our head chef's food last summer, but she rarely made appearances. She and her team have worked hard to prepare the food you see before you, and before we dig in, I convinced her to come out and at least say hello. Lucia, can you come out here?"

Mason's eyes shifted to the side entrance. He, like most of the other players, had been curious as to who this amazing chef was. The door opened and a petite woman with dark hair and olive skin stepped through.

Next to him, he heard Jefferson suck in a breath, and he turned to look at him. "You okay?"

"She's gorgeous," Jefferson whispered.

Mason smiled. Perhaps if things went well, Jefferson might be the next one of them to settle down with a wonderful woman.

The woman stopped next to the coach and lifted a hand shyly. "Hello, I am Lucia. I'm originally from Italy, but I am enjoying cooking for all of you. Congratulations to the happy couple. I hope you enjoy the food." Her voice was friendly, but her eyes were wide and round as if the sight of so many people terrified her. With her spiel finished, she flashed another wave and hurried back out the way she came.

"She seems very shy," Clara said.

"But boy can she cook," Mason said. "Come on, I think they're waiting for us to start the line."

Mason filled his plate with more than he could possibly eat and suggested Clara do the same. They wouldn't clean their plates, but there was no way he wasn't trying a bite of everything. When everyone had their food, Blaine led them in a prayer and then everyone dug in. For a moment there was silence as everyone chewed and then the conversation started again.

"You're right. This food is amazing," Clara said.

Mason smiled and took a moment to watch her enjoy the food. He never would have believed seven months ago that Clara would not only come back into his life but agree to be his partner for the rest of it.

She paused, her fork almost to her mouth, as she caught him staring at her. "What? Do I have food on my face?"

"No," he shook his head, "you're beautiful. I just can't believe I finally get to marry you tomorrow."

She smiled back, set her fork down, and placed her hand on his. "I've always heard that the best things are worth waiting for. I never agreed with that before, but I think they may just be right."

Mason did too. As he looked around the room at their reconciled families and their friends, he knew that tomorrow would be just the start of the best years of his life.

The End!

IF YOU LOVED CLARA AND MASON'S STORY, I WOULD LOVE it if you would leave a review. It helps others take a chance on my books!

And if you want to know what Jefferson is hiding and what's in store for him, be sure to pre-order Second Chance Reception now!

❧ 27 ❧

NOT READY TO SAY GOODBYE
YET?

TOUCHDOWN ON LOVE IS THE FOURTH BOOK IN THE TEXAS Tornado series. Continue the journey with Second Chance Reception— Jefferson's story

Second Chance Reception

He's the wide receiver who's hiding something.

She's the new team cook who rarely shows herself.

Can they find their way to each other or will their secrets keep them apart?

CLICK HERE TO PREORDER SECOND CHANCE RECEPTION AND turn the page for a special sneak peek.

28

A FREE STORY FOR YOU

Enjoyed this story? Not ready to quit reading yet? If you sign up for my newsletter, you will receive The Billionaire's Impromptu Bet right away as my thank you gift for choosing to hang out with me.

The Billionaire's Impromptu Bet

A SWAT officer. A bored billionaire heiress. A bet that could change everything....

Read on for a taste of The Billionaire's Impromptu Bet....

29

THE BILLIONAIRE'S IMPROMPTU BET PREVIEW

Brie Carter fell back spread eagle on her queen-sized canopy bed sending her blonde hair fanning out behind her. With a large sigh, she uttered, "I'm bored."

"How can you be bored? You have like millions of dollars." Her friend, Ariel, plopped down in a seated position on the bed beside her and flicked her raven hair off her shoulder. "You want to go shopping? I hear Tiffany's is having a special right now."

Brie rolled her eyes. Shopping? Where was the excitement in that? With her three platinum cards, she could go shopping whenever she wanted. "No, I'm bored with shopping too. I have everything. I want to do something exciting. Something we don't normally do."

Brie enjoyed being rich. She loved the unlimited credit

cards at her disposal, the constant apparel of new clothes, and of course the penthouse apartment her father paid for, but lately, she longed for something more fulfilling.

Ariel's hazel eyes widened. "I know. There's a new bar down on Franklin Street. Why don't we go play a little game?"

Brie sat up, intrigued at the secrecy and the twinkle in Ariel's eyes. "What kind of game?"

"A betting game. You let me pick out any man in the place. Then you try to get him to propose to you."

Brie wrinkled her nose. "But I don't want to get married." She loved her freedom and didn't want to share her penthouse with anyone, especially some man.

"You don't marry him, silly. You just get him to propose."

Brie bit her lip as she thought. It had been awhile since her last relationship and having a man dote on her for a month might be interesting, but…. "I don't know. It doesn't seem very nice."

"How about I sweeten the pot? If you win, I'll set you up on a date with my brother."

Brie cocked her head. Was she serious? The only thing Brie couldn't seem to buy in the world was the affection of Ariel's very handsome, very wealthy, brother. He was a movie star, just the kind of person Brie could consider marrying in the future. She'd had a crush on him as long as she and Ariel had been friends, but he'd always seen her as just that, his little sister's friend. "I thought you didn't want me dating your brother."

"I don't." Ariel shrugged. "But he's between girlfriends right now, and I know you've wanted it for ages. If you win this bet, I'll set you up. I can't guarantee any more than one date though. The rest will be up to you."

Brie wasn't worried about that. Charm she possessed in abundance. She simply needed some alone time with him, and she was certain she'd be able to convince him they were meant to be together. "All right. You've got a deal."

Ariel smiled. "Perfect. Let's get you changed then and see who the lucky man will be."

A tiny tug pulled on Brie's heart that this still wasn't right, but she dismissed it. This was simply a means to an end, and he'd never have to know.

JESSE CALHOUN RELAXED AS THE RHYTHMIC THUDDING OF the speed bag reached his ears. Though he loved his job, it was stressful being the SWAT sniper. He hated having to take human lives and today had been especially rough. The team had been called out to a drug bust, and Jesse was forced to return fire at three hostiles. He didn't care that they fired at his team and himself first. Taking a life was always hard, and every one of them haunted his dreams.

"You gonna bust that one too?" His co-worker Brendan

appeared by his side. Brendan was the opposite of Jesse in nearly every way. Where Jesse's hair was a dark copper, Brendan's was nearly black. Jesse sported paler skin and a dusting of freckles across his nose, but Brendan's skin was naturally dark and freckle free.

Jesse flashed a crooked grin, but kept his eyes on the small, swinging black bag. The speed bag was his way to release, but a few times he had started hitting while still too keyed up and he had ruptured the bag. Okay, five times, but who was counting really? Besides, it was a better way to calm his nerves than other things he could choose. Drinking, fights, gambling, women.

"Nah, I think this one will last a little longer." His shoulders began to burn, and he gave the bag another few punches for good measure before dropping his arms and letting it swing to a stop. "See? It lives to be hit at least another day." Every once in a while, Jesse missed training the way he used to. Before he joined the force, he had been an amateur boxer, on his way to being a pro, but a shoulder injury had delayed his training and forced him to consider something else. It had eventually healed, but by then he had lost his edge.

"Hey, why don't you come drink with us?" Brendan clapped a hand on Jesse's shoulder as they headed into the locker room.

"You know I don't drink." Jesse often felt like the outsider of the team. While half of the six-man team was married, the other half found solace in empty bottles and meaningless relationships. Jesse understood that — their job was such that they never knew if they would come home night after night — but he still couldn't partake.

Brendan opened his locker and pulled out a clean shirt. He peeled off his current one and added deodorant before tugging on the new one. "You don't have to drink. Look, I won't drink either. Just come and hang out with us. You have no one waiting for you at home."

That wasn't entirely true. Jesse had Bugsy, his Boston Terrier, but he understood Brendan's point. Most days, Jesse went home, fed Bugsy, made dinner, and fell asleep watching TV on the couch. It wasn't much of a life. "All right, I'll go, but I'm not drinking."

Brendan's lips pulled back to reveal his perfectly white teeth. He bragged about them, but Jesse knew they were veneers. "That's the spirit. Hurry up and change. We don't want to leave the rest of the team waiting."

"Is everyone coming?" Jesse pulled out his shower necessities. Brendan might feel comfortable going out with just a new application of deodorant, but Jesse needed to wash more than just dirt and sweat off. He needed to wash the sound of the bullets and the sight of lifeless bodies from his mind.

"Yeah, Pat's wife is pregnant again and demanding some crazy food concoctions. Pat agreed to pick them up if she let him have an hour. Cam and Jared's wives are having a girls' night, so the whole gang can be together. It will be nice to hang out when we aren't worried about being shot at."

"Fine. Give me ten minutes. Unlike you, I like to clean up before I go out."

Brendan smirked. "I've never had any complaints. Besides, do you know how long it takes me to get my hair like this?"

Jesse shook his head as he walked into the shower, but he knew it was true. Brendan had rugged good looks and muscles to match. He rarely had a hard time finding a woman. Jesse on the other hand hadn't dated anyone in the last few months. It wasn't that he hadn't been looking, but he was quieter than his teammates. And he wasn't looking for right now. He was looking for forever. He just hadn't found it yet.

Click here to continue reading The Billionaire's Impromptu Bet.

THE STORY DOESN'T END!

You've met a few people and fallen in love....

I bet you're wondering how you can meet everyone else.

Star Lake Series:

When Love Returns: Can Presley and Brandon forget past hurts or will their stubborn natures keep them apart forever?

Once Upon a Star: Now that Blake has gained confidence and some muscle, will he finally be able to reveal his feelings to Audrey?

Love Conquers All: Now that Azarius has another chance with Laney, will he find the courage to share his life with her? Or will his emotional walls create a barrier that will leave him alone once more?

The Heartbeats Series:

Where It All Began: Will Sandra tell Henry her darkest secret? And will she ever be able to forgive herself and find healing? Find out in this emotional love story.

The Power of Prayer: Who will Callie choose and how will her choice affect the rest of her life? Find out in this touching novel.

When Hearts Collide: Amanda captivates his heart, but can Jared save her from making the biggest mistake of her life? A must read for mothers and daughters.

A Past Forgiven: Can Chad leave his bad-boy image behind and step up and be there for Jess and the baby?

Sweet Billionaires Series:

The Billionaire's Secret: Can Max really change his philandering ways? Or will one mistake seal his fate forever?

A Brush with a Billionaire: Will Brent and Sam's stubborn natures keep them apart or can a small town festival bring them together?

The Billionaire's Christmas Miracle: Drew Devonshire is captivated by the woman he meets at a masquerade ball, but who is she?

The Billionaire's Cowboy Groom: When Carrie returns to town requesting a divorce, can he convince her they belong together?

The Cowboy Billionaire: Coming Soon!

The Lawkeeper Series:

Lawfully Matched: Will Jesse find his fiancee's killer?

And when Kate flies into his life, will he be able to put his painful past behind him in order to love again?

Lawfully Justified: Can Emma offer William a reason to stay? Can William find a way to heal from his broken past to start a future with Emma? Or will a haunting secret take away all the possibilities of this budding romance?

The Scarlet Wedding: William and Emma are planning their wedding, but an outbreak and a return from his past force them to change their plans. Is a happily ever after still in their future?

Lawfully Redeemed: Dani Higgins is a K9 cop looking to make a name for herself, but she finds herself at the mercy of a stranger after an accident. Calvin Phillips just wanted to help his brother, but somehow he ended up in the middle of a police investigation and caring for the woman trying to bring his brother in.

The Still Small Voice Series:

The Still Small Voice: Will Kat be able to give up control and do what God is asking of her?

A Spark in the Darkness coming soon!

Blushing Brides Series:

The Cowboy's Reality Bride: Laney Swann has been running from her past for years, but it takes meeting a man on a reality dating show to make her see there's no need to run.

The Reality Bride's Baby: Laney wants nothing more than a baby, but when she starts feeling dizzy is it pregnancy or something more serious?

The Producer's Unlikely Bride: Ava McDermott is waiting for the perfect love, but after agreeing to a fake relationship with Justin, she finds herself falling for real.

Ava's Blessing in Disguise: Five years after marriage, Ava faces a mysterious illness that threatens to ruin her career. Will she find out what it is?

The Soldier's Steadfast Bride: coming soon

The Men of Fire Beach

Fire Games: Cassidy returns home from Who Wants to Marry a Cowboy to find obsessive letters from a fan. The cop assigned to help her wants to get back to his case, but what she sees at a fire may just be the key he's looking for.

Lost Memories and New Beginnings: She has no idea who she is. He's the doctor caring for her. When her past collides with his present, can he keep her safe?

When Questions Abound A companion story to Lost Memories, this book tells the story from Detective Jordan Graves's point of view.

Never Forget the Past

Secrets and Suspense coming soon!

Stand Alones:

Love Renewed: This books is part of the multi author second chance series. When fate reunites high school sweethearts separated by life's choices, can they find a second chance at love at a snowy lodge amid a little mystery?

Her children's early reader chapter book series:

The Wishing Stone #1: Dangerous Dinosaur
The Wishing Stone #2: Dragon Dilemma
The Wishing Stone #3: Mesmerizing Mermaids
The Wishing Stone #4: Pyramid Puzzle
The Wishing Stone Inspirations 1: Mary's Miracle
To see a list of all her books

authorloranahoopes.com
loranahoopes@gmail.com

DISCUSSION QUESTIONS

1. What was your favorite scene in the book? What made it your favorite?

2. Did you have a favorite line in the book? What do you think made it so memorable?

3. Who was your favorite character in the book and why?

4. Mason faced issues of pride in the book. Do you struggle with pride?

5. What do you think would be the hardest part about dating a celebrity?

6. What did you learn about God from reading this book?

7. How can you use that knowledge in your life from now on?

8. What can you take away from Mason and Clara's relationship?

9. What do you think would make the story even better?